STORYTELLER

Nicholas Bylotas

Savant Books and Publications
Honolulu, HI, USA
2017

Published in the USA by Savant Books and Publications
2630 Kapiolani Blvd #1601
Honolulu, HI 96826
http://www.savantbooksandpublications.com

Printed in the USA

Edited by D. T. Wolfe
Cover by Daniel S. Janik
Cover Image: keyhole-door-handle-1763200 by Maaark | Pixabay.com

13 digit ISBN: 978-0-9972472-6-8

First Edition: October 2017
Library of Congress Control Number: 2017953865

Dedication

to the Living and the Dead

Acknowledgements

I humbly acknowledge with my everlasting gratitude, the corpus of minds and bodies, both living and dead, who terrorized and bolstered me during the creation of this work. Thank you for appearing in my consciousness – from wherever in the cosmos you are. Thank you, Satan, and all your infernal kingdom. May my suffering people, condemned by false leaders to an eternity in Hell, be relieved by the medicinal properties contained within this work. Thank you, beloved Hive Queen, and all the denizens of the natural world, whose ancient wisdom has been a companion and teacher most fundamental to my happiness. To the Teeming Dead, whose spirits are the firmament in which I have climbed to better see reality from, thank you. Lastly, ye who will not be named, hoping to hear your own self proclaimed back from the universe, I thank thee most graciously.

PART I

Nicholas Bylotas

Chapter 1 - Once Upon a Time…

Deserts were familiar to Vaks, and even here in the bleakness and desolation at the end of things, there was an odd comfort in the whipping sand and beating wind that assaulted his lonely walk. The effects of thirst and hunger were creeping into his brain, and compounded with the haunting terror of his waking nightmares, he was rapidly losing the ability to differentiate between the Story and reality.

The Story bubbled up in his mind like twisted memories tainted with the black oil of Entropy, their faces stretching out from a thin membrane of shadows, limbs pushing upward against the film of consciousness like the spines of a writhing leviathan, hungry to eat.

Faces swirled from piles of sand underneath the blackened shrubs that grew without leaf or color. Their sandy mouths reminded him with taunts and jeers of all that he had lost and left behind.

His fingers found the empty vial strung around his neck. There was no going back. Why he still held onto the glass, he didn't know, but there was something reassuring about carrying the vessel with him, allowing it to contain the grief of his loss.

His head hung down from the weight of psychological oppression—undefinable, untreatable, and uncontrollable—yet his body trudged on, unwilling to die. There was, after all, another StoryTeller left alive.

Shammal had confessed it before he died, Vaks having caught up to him with savage ferocity, and exacting his vengeance without mercy. He was driven by bloodlust, and without a living person he knew left, nor a past to go back to, he swallowed the terminal dose of Sand that brought him beyond Time itself, a place no StoryTeller had ever returned from.

The shift across spacetime was uncomfortable to the untrained, but Vaks was exceptional in his ability, and manifested into reality in stride, running at full length toward his quarry, the murderer of his tribe.

He was addled already by the hallucinations that had begun to appear on Jal and with the utter insanity of holding his infant son's lifeless corpse in his hands; he hunted like no StoryTeller had ever hunted before.

Entropy urged him on with the fiery tongues of encouragement and, without rest, he ran after his prey day and night, loping through the darkness. By the breaking dawn's crimson light, he came upon the killer's lonely camp.

The small flame he was kneeling beside was the only star in the blackness, for there were none left at the Edge of Time, and it too would be snuffed out when Vaks reached its creator.

Shammal was surprised to see Vaks, thinking he had killed everyone at the Halls of Remembrance, frowning that he had missed one, since he so meticulously ensured everyone was dead.

When Vaks appeared from the darkness, he was panting and sweaty from his pursuit, wildly charging through the desert with complete disregard for his survival. He removed his hood. Dark eyes glowered from under the shadows of his brow, the curls of his dark, wet hair adhering to his forehead.

The moment of awareness was a lightning strike that happened the instant their eyes contacted over the flames. No time could be spared on words for Vaks, and he leapt forward across the flame, leading his knee into the gaping face of Shammal.

Blood arced from Shammal as he was flung backwards, unable to retrieve his weapon or activate his stealth. Vaks drew his blade and held it to the man's throat, the unshaven stubble bristling under the knife's edge. Vaks could smell the blood of his people on him and was driven beyond reason to such an extent that no words could find voice; he snarled and roared, spittle flying from his mouth, his knuckles white and trembling.

Shammal laughed and Vaks hit him across the jaw. Shammal laughed still, his own madness meeting Vaks entirely.

"You can't kill me, StoryTeller," the man sneered through hysterical bleeding guffaws. "I can never be killed by you!"

Vaks, his knees pressed on the man's shoulders, pinning him with the knife at the throat, gripped a fistful of Shammal's hair and pulled his face close.

Entropy itself peered of out of those infernal portals to his soul and, for an instant, Shammal quivered. Vaks drew the blade across Shammal's brow, forcibly holding him still with supernatural adrenal strength as Shammal howled with pain and fear.

With one savage rip, Vaks separated the scalp from Shammal's head and held it up in the moonlight. Shammal mumbled with tears and submission as Vaks admired his trophy and looked down at his prey. "If you wish any matter of yourself to be redeemed, tell me: Why did you kill my people?" Vaks asked.

Vaks now held the man's head from underneath the jaw, sand congealing with the blood on his skull. Still Shammal uttered a weak laugh. "A StoryTeller sent me, O savage one!" he said, spitting a glob of blood and mucus into Vaks' face and shrieking maniacally.

It was more than Vaks was willing to bear, and he squeezed the man's throat, cutting off his laughter and bulging the eyes. With a full view of what was inside Shammal's eyes, Vaks plunged the knife slowly into his heart, and leaned close with malevolent pleasure as the trace of life left his quarry.

That was three days ago. Vaks had nowhere to go but onward, since all around him was the vastness of the desert. With each day, the sun and moon seemed to rise from a different direction, giving him no course to follow, except toward where his feet pulled him.

He didn't fear the prospect of dying, but could not give up when the Story was still being told. If there was a StoryTeller who had commissioned the mass murder of his own tribe, Vaks would not rest until he closed the tale.

There was no denying the compulsions that had been crafted into his genetic material over generations of StoryTelling. His need to conclude the mystery was as vital to his life as was breath to the uninitiated. Autonomously his body compelled him forward, while his mind wanted death.

He had lost Shiela. He had failed as a StoryTeller. Now he was a murderer, and there was no one left alive that could help him, the StoryTellers themselves being from a realm now inaccessible. The Halls of Remembrance, that mighty Temple that had once been his home, was stained red with the blood of innocents, and their humble work of recording the Great Story would never be completed.

Vaks certainly wasn't the one to lead the work now. He was likely the worst of them all, and now he was among the final two remaining. There was so much that he would never know now that his masters were killed by Shammal before they could raise him to his final form in the Order of Story. There were secrets they kept, ancient powers of the Art which now were dead with all the Story-Tellers and abandoned books that were once alive in the Halls.

Rattling shook the air, and Vaks shot his gaze ahead of him at the source.

A coiled black snake flicked a pink, forked tongue at him from twenty paces away. Its crimson eyes were fixed in its face as rubies. The tail poised itself upward like the stinger of a scorpion.

Vaks halted and took a breath. It was the first life he had seen since he took the last.

Stepping forward, not changing his course for the sake of keeping his direction of travel, he walked on, half fearing the serpent, half hoping it would bite him.

It rattled more furiously as he approached, the tail reaching higher.

When Vaks was closest to it, the rattling ceased.

Vaks passed on without hesitation or hurry, keeping his pace, and the serpent did not bite him.

His robes had frayed in the desert winds, and the sturdy fabric was revealing a number of loose threads. He reached for his water skin and twisted the cap. Vaks felt the grooves on the pads of his fingers. Before opening it, he knew it was empty. It was an impulsive gesture, and he stopped before he released the evaporated moisture within. Vaks fastened the skin to his waist and fell to a knee with a gasp.

He couldn't walk anymore. He couldn't sleep well enough to rest, or walk on with no water in this heat. His body was shutting down. Vaks ground his teeth, his fingers gripping the dirt as rage poured into him. Dry tears forced their way into his eyes. He couldn't die now.

Entropy approached him, sliding a curved claw across the surface of Vaks' skull, dragging electricity along its path. He lifted his head up and looked into the shadowy mask of Entropy. The shadows could never hold a single form for long, and through a changing amalgamation of features, they swirled together as if the Stygian waters were contained in a single body. There the souls of the damned swam frantically about within that blackness just for a chance to see the light of the surface.

Two mandibles protruded outward, and from the inky blackness, thin spider-like arms sprouted in different directions, two of them gripping Vaks at the temples, pulling him into morbidity.

When Vaks awoke, a locust was perched on the back of his hand. He looked at it hungrily and it leapt away.

The sun was setting and the moon rising, each arriving as always with perfect timing. On the horizon a thin column of smoke rose from a speck. Vaks gradually made his way to his feet, and pressed toward it, shambling with the dregs of strength that remained. The sight of smoke brought him energy and his pace increased.

He could see the speck now. A house perhaps?

He stumbled on and saw that it was the prospect of salvation raining down upon him. There was no water left to cry, nor wind to spare for shouting. Vaks crossed the remaining distance with delirium and fear.

The porch was a single step to climb and Vaks could hardly muster the strength to do so. When he reached the door, he could hear the creaking of a chair rocking back and forth inside.

Lifting a hand, he brought it down as a fist, announcing his arrival with a solemn and final thud. There was no strength to lift his hand again. When he heard the click of a bolt action rifle inside, the doom caused by its sound took the last of his will.

Vaks would die here, as would any man, because at the Edge of Time only the bitter, the shrewd, and the evil survive. The door opened inward when Vaks was leaning his full weight against it.

He collapsed onto the wooden floorboards, the shot of the rifle forcing its way out. His chin collided with the floor, and he winced, thanking himself that he was still alive. The bullet must have missed.

"Oh, fuck!" Vaks heard the man say, and then felt himself being turned over. He looked into the face of his rescuer, his blurry vision unable to parse out details.

"Wa…t…" Vaks could not articulate the word through his hoarse voice, but the man understood anyway and retrieved a skin of water, administering it to Vaks' lips.

The cooling pain was exquisite, and Vaks gripped the water skin and greedily slaked his thirst. He once looked at the man with shameful eyes, but the man only shook his head and encouraged him to drink his fill.

Vaks' vision was returning, and he could only distinguish the curled black mustache on the man's face before darkness started settling in. His head rolled over to the side and the blood stains on the man's cowboy boots initiated the nightmare that followed.

Chapter 2 - Cartin Delgado

Spring was coming in. Not that it meant much up in the Needle Edges. There just weren't many living plants in that place. There was a cactus species that would sprout an occasional red flower, and spiny, brittle shrubs, but not much more.

"Pay attention," Cartin's grandmother told her once as she plucked the brittle leaves from a plant and deposited them into a pouch. "These leaves will help fend off nightmares if you drink them in a tea."

It still made Cartin sad to remember her grandmother, even if she seldom needed to use her natural remedies. Cartin was strong and healthy. She was a mining girl; one of the best, too. A lot of the guys couldn't keep up with her. Despite her size, she was tremendously capable and proved herself to be deft with a Pick.

They weren't all miners in Vastrix, however. That was just the mission of the colony. Cantor needed the minerals from the land to fund the rest of civilization. Cantor was the capital of all remaining human and alien society, and ever since the A.I. turned on humanity, the surviving humans came together in the only inhabitable region left on this side of the planet. No one had been in contact with the other side since. Not that people didn't have access to the kind of technology that could navigate through the oceans, but they didn't know how to use it without the A.I.

Cartin Delgado was thinking about her sixteenth birthday. It was today. No one took birthdays off or anything, but it was still generally noted among the other miners when someone was celebrating a new year. There were a lot of unexpected deaths in the Needles, especially underneath the Needles.

It was dangerous to be a miner before the A.I. had turned, as her grandmother had told her, but much more so now, in Cartin's opinion. Grandma Delgado was only a girl when it happened anyway, and Cartin recalled only a faint memory of her father coming home with boots sooty with blue dust from the mines. The same blue dust that clung to his callused hands as he messed up her hair.

Cartin Delgado hadn't really known how hard it was back then, but she was sure that they didn't have mutant bats to deal with. Sure, they had gotten pretty good at killing them now, but when they drilled into a cavern with a hive of mine bats, it was never an easy day. Someone was always taken.

They might have taken Cartin the other day. She was mining through a new passage, dancing to the music she made with the Pick. The hiss of the cylinders, the steam of the pipes, and the squeal of the stone as the philosteel tip melted through it. It was music she made with the full intention of doing so, and she used every bit of concentration to pull it off. It was the music they all made. She was just so young to have already found the music of the mines in herself that it took all her effort to make it.

When the miners do their work, what comes from the caverns is the symphony of humanity. Or at least the humanity that Cartin was aware of. They never got many visitors to the Needles, and those born there rarely left. When one person did leave to seek a better life in a different land, it put such a burden on the rest of the people that it was highly discouraged and considered the greatest disgrace.

Cartin had no intention of leaving. In fact, she felt most alive when she was making music with her Pick. The coordination of levers, hydraulic pressure, and torque levels was difficult to manage for most, but when Cartin inherited hers, the music came to her as naturally as a supplement to her spoken language.

She crashed through stone and broke into a bubble, waking up a wild mine bat. It was one of the ones that took off on its own. One of those that always became the most vicious. One that escaped the hive. Cartin leapt backward and teeth scraped against teeth as she thrust her Pick between herself and the bat. Cartin fell as the bat swooped upon her.

She hadn't had time to gasp. Another Pick crashed into the whipping leather wings of the beast and squashed its torso into the earthen walls, drilling the bloody carcass into stone.

Rickard was there. He had seen her mine into the cavern. He had been watching her. It was hard not to watch her. Practically every guy did. She was a capable miner and loved her work so much that her enthusiasm spread to the others. The men, however, were mostly concerned with her as an eligible mate, and Rickard was no exception.

The blood of the mangled beast had splashed onto her blue and orange coveralls, hairy pulp from its meat clinging to the stone. Rickard extended a hand to her and helped Cartin up. Her cheeks were red with embarrassment at the assistance, but she was not so impertinent as to be ungrateful. She thanked him with the customary embrace, but when he responded by asking for her hand in marriage, she gently declined.

It wasn't uncommon for the people of Vastrix to marry at sixteen, or even younger in some cases. It wasn't the most frequent practice, but because people died so frequently, young marriages were encouraged.

Cartin blew a strand of black hair out of her face as she slid her weight into the Pick and tore apart a crevice of earth.

She had to turn him down. Even after he had saved her life. Rickard was a great guy and was certainly handsome, but Cartin loved Mikhail. She had loved him ever since they were children playing mutants and cyborgs in school. They always took walks together after their shifts, and when they made the music of the mines, theirs was an undeniable beauty that enchanted even the mumbling old men, whose bodies could no longer wield a Pick.

They worked constantly in the mines, cycling fresh miners with exhausted ones who danced to the music of the mines for sheer pleasure—when they were rested enough to do so. Some even sang. They sang stories about the worlds and peoples long gone. Stories about how the universe was before it ended. Songs of a place that existed long before the Edge of Time was even built.

Cartin wasn't much interested in the way the universe was historically, but she did love to hear the stories about the great heroes of life. Most of them were human, but there were heroes of other species that she knew of, and the aliens always seemed far more advanced than people gave them credit for.

Cartin had learned about Necrodian lore from Mikhail.

Mikhail knew a lot about that stuff, and by spending so much time with him, so did Cartin. He was always telling her stories about the legendary planets whose inhabitants rode machines across the sky that could dive into the depths of the oceans and do battle with the monsters of shadow. He never liked to tell the stories about the great romances that brought galaxies together though.

Cartin always had to ask him to tell those stories. He'd usually sigh and give her a sly smile, acquiescing to tell the story. She noticed the way he brightened when she asked him, and Cartin knew, by that virtue, that he loved the romances, too.

"Cartin?"

She nearly dropped her Pick.

"Hey!"

"Sorry, I didn't mean to startle you."

Mikhail shouldn't be here right now. He worked in a completely different annex of the mine. It was one of the exploratory mines. One of the ones that delved into the lost shafts after the A.I. rebellion. When the robots revolted, the collateral damage from the severe earthquakes that destroyed the planetary stabilizing systems spewed radioactive material throughout the biosphere. Nearly every mining colony was lost to either collapsing overheads or violent mutations. Mikhail's stories of his explorative missions were so horrific that she often considered her encounters with mine bats trivial.

It was important work he was doing. There was a lot of salvageable equipment in the mines. He had told her about some interesting artifacts they had found in some of them. Old books that showed depictions of StoryTellers telling their strange mythology.

Cartin didn't know why people would be so foolish as to believe some nonsense like that, but then again, she could believe anything was possible if this was really the end of it all. The universe had long faded, having collapsed into itself. This single planet, this epitaph of life, an engineered world known as the Edge of Time, was the only form of existence that managed to escape the Ragnarok Wave.

Now it was coming to an end. Cartin knew it. Mikhail knew it. Every conscious creature alive knew it. It was the time remaining that the gravity core could hold sustainment after the A.I. had corrupted the architecture. It was a countdown. There had never been any technology greater than the Edge of Time, and there never would be. Its end marked the extinction of the beloved gift of consciousness that was bio-technology.

Someone had analyzed the systems with reasonable accuracy and predicted a survival range of 76 years and 266 days. Cartin wasn't much bothered by this news. She'd have mostly lived a whole life by then, or would have died happily beforehand from a glorious mining catastrophe or from battle with a mutant otherwise.

"What were you thinking about?" Mikhail asked.

"I was..." Cartin scrunched her nose. "I was thinking about... well, you."

Mikhail stepped to Cartin and brought her close to his body. She nearly dropped the Pick, but held onto it beside them. Her arm strained with the weight, but the way he was holding her was so powerful she felt like she could do anything.

Mikhail drew her gaze. "Cartin Delgado, muse of the mines, fire to my music— be my wife."

He looked into her eyes as she had long dreamed he would look at her.

"Yes!"

He laughed triumphantly and kissed her, both of them dropping their Picks. Her fingers lingered on his cheeks.

"When?" she asked.

"This moon," he answered, kissing her lips. "It will be full in three days. Can you be ready by then?"

"I'd have to get a dress..."

"That's fine. I can schedule another time, but it will be a few weeks."

"No!" Cartin exclaimed and then blushed. "I mean, I can be ready in three days."

Chapter 3 - Javier Estolla

When Vaks awoke, he was surprised by his restfulness. He was not sure how long he had been asleep. It might have been days with the way his blisters looked.

Across the room sat a brown-skinned man with a cowboy hat rolling a cigarette. His shirt was patterned blue. His boots were brown. There were gray hairs streaking the mustache that waxed into curls above his lips.

"Care for a smoke?" the man called across the room.

The voice crawled its way into Vaks' awareness and rose him up.

"Yes," Vaks said after some time. "Thank you."

As Vaks stood, he saw that his belongings were lain neatly beside the cot. The hilt of the knife gleamed out of the folds of leather, reminding him of a darker truth. Reminding him of Entropy.

Vaks could sense him nearby. He wasn't present in his monstrous form, but he was still present nonetheless.

His eyes darted toward movement. Within the shadows of an ajar closet door across the room was a darkness that beheld the boding terror of two yellow eyes. There lurked the thing.

Entropy was here. Entropy was always here. Vaks swallowed

grimly and stretched his spine upward with his head as he made his way over.

As Vaks sat down, the man tucked the cigarette firmly in place and offered it to Vaks with his right hand while reaching for the herbs with his left.

Vaks reached for the matchbox on the table and struck a flame. Dry crackling herbs burned into his lungs and were osmosed into his blood, delighting him. The smoke plumed upward as relief, satisfaction, and harmony flooded into Vaks' mind.

He was safe.

The man remained silent as he deftly finished rolling another cigarette and struck it lit. They sat in silence as the smoke drifted in calm gray lines across the yellow plane of morning light.

"Where ya headed?"

The words strummed like a guitar through the desert quiet.

"I'm after a StoryTeller," Vaks said.

The man took a long drag from his cigarette, the orange cherry flashing bright before he removed it from his mouth.

Exhaling, he said, "Son, if you're looking for a StoryTeller, I reckon you might be one yourself."

Vaks tensed. His skin prickled with the rush of nicotine and something else. His eyes widened and his pulse quickened.

"That I am."

The man's eyes widened with surprise, and he leaned forward, exhaling his smoke behind him. "You mean, for real?"

Vaks nodded.

The man took another drag from his cigarette. He offered his hand out. "Name's Javier Estolla. Pleased to meet ya."

"Vaks Biblent."

He had a firm handshake, not aggressive. "Thank you for saving my life."

"Not a problem, friend. Mi casa es su casa."

Vaks wasn't sure what to make of that. The Spanish colonies were known to have merged with the intergalactic speaking technique ages ago. The IST enables the speakers and listeners to communicate with each other in the best language their brains understand.

It was a technique developed by the StoryTellers so they could communicate with the rest of humanity. It was extraordinarily helpful when they appeared around the universe, seeking memories to record into the Pools—or when they needed to get directions. The rest of humanity had adapted to the technique from communicating with StoryTellers by proximity. It was an unanticipated effect for the StoryTellers, but one that proved invaluable to life everywhere.

Vaks still had not heard a Spanish dialect in a very long time. Not since he visited one of the Child Planets.

"Again, thank you. But I beseech you: Do you know of a StoryTeller who dwells among these lands?"

Javier had a puzzled look on his face. "Sure..." He must have seen something grave in Vaks' eyes because his own expression became the visage of doom. "I believe there is one out there, though I can't say where."

Vaks smiled, but closed his eyes in contemplation as he sighed gently.

"I am sure they'll know in Cantor, though."

The man's words were so abrupt that Vaks was unsure of whether or not he could trust Javier Estolla.

That however, was a stigma Vaks carried his whole life, culminated into its fullness now. He didn't trust any people. Not only because he had been betrayed most painfully by the woman he loved, but also because there was no one left alive who knew him. They had all died under Shammal's malevolent hand.

"Will you show me the way there?" Vaks asked.

"I will." The man twisted his mustache. "On one condition."

"What's that?"

"You have to tell me *your* story."

Vaks' eyes widened. He inhaled sharply. That was a line he had never crossed. The Individual Story was everything the Order fought to protect in the universe. By telling it, it was put at risk, resulting in an unforgivable offense. Not even Vaks had broken that rule in his years. The penalty was death—or numbness.

Chapter 4 - Jal

Four years earlier...

Vaks appeared through the portal of Sand with a gasp. It came as a surprise every time, and felt like being pulled inside out through the exit. He was used to the sensation however, and set about exploring the forest around him without a moment's hesitation.

You never knew what you were going to get when you were summoned to a Story, and here Vaks found himself, to his delight, on a beautiful, lush world, and in the prime of his life.

A young man, more experienced both in life and love than most people his age, Vaks was an extraordinary individual. His childhood was notoriously marked with infractions and reprimands from the Elders due to his "delinquency." But despite this, Vaks was still respected as an adept in the ways of his order, with an unmistakable contribution to their unending work, in a manner none but he could replicate.

He loved his life, his creed, his people more than anything else in the world. Except for the Story that is. Nothing was ever as compelling as the Story to Vaks. Through it, he recognized the cosmic unity that flowed from the same people on many different worlds, not because they looked the same, but because their spirit was a repeating occurrence.

They were the great heroes of Life, the women and men who charged forth and fought evil when it sprouted in a place. Sure as Life gives Life, so the heroes defended to the death that which is dearest throughout time. The Stories recurred again and again with different contexts, and Vaks studied them all. A StoryTeller was there at every moment humanity evolved consciousness, and stored at the Halls of Remembrance was a memory of every critical point in human time.

Alone on the planet Jal and walking through the forest, his body warm from exercise, his face smiling with pleasure, Vaks stepped onto a light trail. It was a fine day on Jal. Thc flowers were in bloom and the air was cleaner than Vaks had ever smelled it. He was truly having a good time.

The trail ended at a hillside, where below Vaks saw a small town of thatched roofs and large gardens. The way down the hillside was steep, but Vaks was deft, and soon he was approaching the outer wall when…

A flash!

PAIN searing through the skull!

RAGE! Boiling magma from a destructive planet!

Vaks stretched his eyes open and groaned, clutching his head at the spot where his pain was most intense. He screamed like a titan, but sounded only as a feeble human.

Beside him a rock had clunked to the earth. He looked at the shrubbery and saw two children crouching behind it.

"Bastards!"

He wanted to murder them.

He quickly convinced himself that it was better to be good if he was going to get involved at all. He smiled to the children as a dark voice laughed in the back of his mind.

The children ran, and Vaks shook his fist screaming, "PUNKS!" with all the rage he could muster into a single blast of acoustic energy. It was a significant amount of rage, making his voice a roar that echoed off the hillside.

The children fled in silence.

Vaks walked on, his seething rage dissipating with each passing step. He took a deep breath and by the time he passed through the outer wall, was relaxed enough to allow the incident to melt into the back of his mind.

A short time later he came upon a woman holding a child to her bosom, singing softly in the sunshine bathing the front lawn of her home. She was beautiful with her rosy complexion and full, wholesome body. She winked at him as he approached, having unavoidably caught his eye, her curiosity peaked.

"What brings you into town, stranger?" the woman asked, cheerfully shifting the baby to a more comfortable position.

"Just traveling through, writing a book," Vaks said, knowing his lie was a faint allusion to a kernel of the truth. "Would you by chance know..." She had amazing breasts. "Of a tavern or inn I might stay at?"

"My eyes are up here, mister! You'd better keep yours on them! Alright!?"

"Excuse me please, but..." His cheeks reddened, but he was not discouraged by her. "Do you know of a tavern or inn I might stay at?"

She frowned and looked at him concerned. Could she see the eroding sanity in his eyes? She nodded with a strange, encouraging look that Vaks had never encountered before, and he realized that he had been chosen for a very special Story.

A StoryTeller did not often choose their next Story to embark upon. They were assigned to specific Stories by the Elders, whose manipulation of the Sands was so advanced they could pair specific StoryTellers to specific events. Vaks didn't understand how this was done, but he was sure that the influence of Stories came through a field of space-time that linked the universe together.

His mission here on Jal was to observe the power transition from a vast network of tribal villages into a single nation state run by a council of high chiefs. This type of Story happened on just about every planet's timeline, but what made this one unique was that Jal was host to a peculiar burgeoning religion. The religious entity that was heading the tribal unification of the planet worshipped Story-Tellers. Vaks was there not only to collect the memory of the event and return home, but to also discourage any association with the religion itself.

"My sister Sheila owns the inn down the road. Hordes and Forks it's called. She's about the only thing keeping that place together since Pa died. One of us had to inherit it. Then, when Frankie passed away, Sheila hasn't been much interested in anything other than work."

"Frankie was her husband?"

The woman nodded. "Name's Ethyl by the way."

"Vaks."

"Tell her I sent you, and she'll put you up for the night. She'll expect you to pay eventually, so don't try and take advantage of her generosity." Ethyl put her hands on her hips. "She can be especially menacing when she goes out with that hulk of hers collecting tabs, and if you still owe her, you might have to suffer some broken thumbs."

"Thank you. I'll tell her you sent me."

Vaks lowered his gaze past her breasts to the two children gripping the folds of her dress, peering from behind her.

"You'll have to excuse the young'uns. They are a bit more wild than most, so I keep them on a short leash."

"Quite alright." The sting of pain was a faint echo in his head. "Just a word for them though: Do not throw rocks at strangers. You don't know what monster you might wake up."

Ethyl paled at the comment, and put her hands defensively on her children's shoulders, hugging them close.

"Thanks again, Ethyl," Vaks said cheerfully, then walked on into town.

There is a strange essence the moment people first meet a StoryTeller on a new world. The merging of realities creates a single pause of flow for an instant, before resuming its normal course with a broader scope of existence.

It got messy when people started asking questions. Vaks had to bend their minds in his favor, but it was a small problem to avoid. A StoryTeller had a store of consciousness influence that could implant stories into a person's mind and make them believe certain things. The only way a StoryTeller could recharge his ability to do this was to hear, or tell, another story. Though the energy received from the two actions was different, and telling Stories was strictly forbidden,Vaks regularly filled his stores however he could, regardless of the restrictions.

The art of conscious manipulation was among the more esoteric of the teachings at the Halls of Remembrance, but it was without a doubt one of the most remarkable subjects. There was a distinct power in the force of human thought. It could in fact be manipulated and changed to achieve real results in the tangible world.

It was forbidden to practice with the derived magic of a told Story, however, due to inevitable intervention that resulted. Despite that, the magic capable with the accrued energy was tremendously useful in navigating the universe as a StoryTeller seeking human experiences.

Vaks was adept at it, and the Elders knew it, but they did not stop him. He was discouraged from following that way, but they did not deny his right to choose it.

As Vaks approached the Hordes and Forks Tavern, he noticed an odd sign that drained his blood. The road forked into a main plaza where a gallows had been built, and a single body draped in red cloth hung dead by the neck. It swayed in the breeze. The head was downcast, the skin gray and mottled, its hair a black tangle of curls falling on its chest.

A raven cawed from a perch above and fluttered down onto the shoulder. It cawed again and started pecking at the eyes.

Vaks shuddered and stepped inside the tavern, approaching the bar.

A burly man was drying a clay mug with a bar towel. Fortunately, it looked clean. He raised an eyebrow at Vaks.

"May I speak to the owner, please?"

The man set down the mug and towel and gripped the edges of the sink as he leaned forward to glare at Vaks. "I swear to God if you health inspectors don't give us a break, I am going to crush your spine before you have a chance to cite us for another violation!"

Vaks didn't drop his gaze. "Your owner, please." He said with a level growling tone.

A vein bulged in the man's head as his complexion reddened with anger. A delicate hand slid onto the man's forearm, and Vaks watched the mound of meat relax onto his bones.

"Relax, Darius. What does he want?" a woman said, presumably Sheila, Ethyl's sister and the tavern owner.

"I just came into town. Your sister mentioned you could set me up with a room."

Sheila narrowed her eyes at him. "What kind of place does she think I am running? She's always sending strays to me. I think she keeps trying to get me to re-marry!"

"I can pay my way by performing for you. My skills are in high demand. I am a..."

"StoryTeller!" an old man shouted with a raspy tobacco-riddled throat.

Vaks froze.

There was a clattering as the man shoved his barstool out of his way and came over toward Vaks, pointing a trembling finger.

"I know it...I know it...I can see it in the air about you! You've come from a faraway place that only StoryTellers can visit. You are the dweller between timelines, the keeper of lifetimes. At last you have come to grace us with your wisdom!" The man lowered his head and clasped his hands by his closed eyes.

Vaks cast a hesitant look at Sheila.

"It's true, isn't it?" she asked.

Vaks nodded. "Though, it is not as serious as our friend makes it sound. I am just a regular guy who likes to tell stories." Quietly, he reached his mind out to see if he could lower the passion by which the man believed in his faith. His consciousness was met by an immutable wall, and his skills were useless to change the man's mind.

"No! The scriptures state you will come and untie the bonds of oppression from our minds and enlighten us before the ending of moments!"

"Look, mister," Vaks said, growing agitated at the man's hysteria. "We aren't any kind of deity or god, so you can get that out of your head right away. There isn't any apocalypse coming either, so you don't have anything to worry about."

Vaks regretted the words immediately upon speaking them. There was a strange flashing in the man's eyes. He nodded, and then shoved his way out of the bar, stumbling drunk into the night.

"Don't mind him," Sheila said. "He just drinks too much. It's a shame their religion even allows them to drink alcohol, but they are very liberal in their policies. He's usually in here preaching some nonsense about the Great Story or about the rumors that come in from the space merchants."

Vaks took a moment to notice the snug green corset around Sheila's torso. Her auburn hair twirled in playful locks over her shoulders and onto her chest. "I can tell stories to pay my way. I have been a valuable service to many places for the people I bring." He said, his tone low.

"By all means!" Sheila exclaimed with a clap of her hands. "Here's a key to your room. It'll be the third one on the right. Third floor."

"Thanks." Vaks accepted the key and their fingertips touched.

They looked at each other for a deep breath. Vaks blushed. "May I have an ale, please?"

Sheila laughed, the delight of her energy bubbling out of her uncontrollably. When she reduced her mirth to a quiet giggle, she filled up a mug with cold, crisp ale. Vaks smiled and took a drink. "Cheers."

Sheila blushed now, and Vaks, for the fear of making his introduction with Sheila more embarrassing and awkward than it already was, moved away from the bar and took a place by the fire.

"So you're one of them fabled StoryTellers, huh?" A gruff man said with the soles of his feet stretched out toward the flames. His socks had a hole in the right foot and his big toe burst out of it. His boots were by his seat, the laces strewn across the wooden planks like roots.

"I am."

The man snorted. "I thought ya'll were just made up."

"We're not; though the religion is."

"Are you going to tell us a story?"

"If you'd like."

"Well don't wait for a bloody invitation or anything. If you got a story to tell, then tell it!"

Vaks took a breath and then a large gulp of ale.

What followed was the very magic that Vaks was sent to deny the existence of. When a StoryTeller tells a story, their memory of the event is transmitted neurally across the room to the listeners, allowing them to experience the memories too. It is a profound and captivating experience.

Others wanted to tell their stories, and Vaks gladly stepped aside to become the audience, lending his gift to the others. Together they shared the joys of human experience, and it wasn't long before the tavern was full of patrons. The man who had threatened Vaks at the bar was hustling back and forth with new casks of wine and barrels of ale. Sheila, a beauty reveling in the business, laughed as she observed it all.

She had dispatched a young child to go and tell the other citizens that a StoryTeller was in the tavern. So also did the old man tell his fanatic brethren that a StoryTeller had arrived, and soon, when he reached the border of the capital city to the south, he told the council that ruled the nations. There, in their dark chambers, they began to conspire.

A musical note pierced through the cacophony of voices, laughter, and clinking glasses. Silence settled and Vaks looked at Sheila, standing nearby with her foot on the seat of a chair, a fiddle at her shoulder.

Everyone in the room let their gaze fall on her as she played. Sheila's notes built with tremors of pain and beauty. There was a haunting fluidity to the way her music drifted about the air, each wave a pleasure of poignant experience. Vaks felt his memory drink in the moment and archive it. With it came the euphoria of awareness.

Sheila was also telling a story.

Through the wordlessness of her music, Vaks felt the sorrow of great loss and the simultaneous exuberance of Life, resulting in the harmonies that mesmerized him. It was not long before tears were streaming down his face.

He knew, clear as an epiphany, that he had come all this way in life to fall in love.

Chapter 5 - Whiskey

"You're telling me you came all the way out here because you're lovesick over a girl?" Javier exclaimed.

Vaks gave him a sullen look.

"Oh, come on now, don't be like that! I want to hear more of your story. What happened next?"

"I stayed on Jal," Vaks said.

Javier raised an eyebrow. "And did what?"

"Married Sheila."

There was a heavy silence in the air, and Javier stood up. "I'm going to get some whiskey. I've been saving a bottle for a special occasion. I reckon this one's gonna do it."

He retrieved a bottle of whiskey from the top shelf of a cabinet behind the bar, grabbed two glasses, and sat down again. He twisted out the cork on the whiskey bottle and filled the glasses with stout amber liquid. Vaks accepted the offered glass with a smile, though his eyes still held a sullen darkness.

"Thank you," Vaks said.

"Thank you," Javier said, tilting his glass. "I know what it means for a StoryTeller to tell his story. I have studied your histories. The Annex of Consciousness is the single greatest historical record remaining in existence."

"The Annex of Consciousness?"

Javier looked surprised. "You've never heard of it?" Vaks shrugged, and Javier continued in stride. "They were written by StoryTellers who confessed their stories after being banished as mutes. It's a fascinating history."

Vaks had never heard of the Annex of Consciousness before. He was aware that there were muted StoryTellers, condemned to live their lives in silence, numb to the Sands, but he had never considered before that they would write down their own memories. "Then you know we are sent to places with specific purposes, right? That we leave as abruptly as we arrive and as seamlessly as possible?"

Javier nodded.

"Well, I ignored my purpose for a full year as I spent all my time telling stories at the tavern with Sheila, and we made such a profit that she bought the place outright, and we married to celebrate. Things had begun to get a little crazy though. The word of me being a StoryTeller was spreading pretty drastically across the land too... though I didn't know it at the time."

"And there was that terrible disaster too!" Javier interjected. "The nation consumed itself! It killed every one of its own citizens in the fanatical pursuit of their cult. They were particularly violent and brutal in their judgments toward heretics." Javier looked pale. "I've learned of Jal's history. It is one of the darker subjects of research. Frankly," Javier swallowed the remainder of his whiskey and exhaled, squinting his eyes, "I'm frightened by the fact that you are even telling me a story about it at all."

Javier shuddered. "It's one of the mysteries of humanity. No one knows what really happened there. The only images we have are of the dead. An entire planet...sacrificed."

Vaks stared at him blankly, the strangeness of the coincidence rooting into his brain.

He had left Entropy out of the story. Javier didn't need to know that Vaks was hallucinating. He didn't need to know that even now the shadows of the universe were breathing with life of their own.

"Jesus!" Javier exclaimed.

Vaks smirked when he heard the traditional blasphemy. It was one of his personal favorites. "What's wrong?"

"I...don't know. I guess I saw something in your eyes, but I can't quite describe it."

"Entropy is what you saw," Vaks said. "It's here. It's why the universe swallowed itself. Ever since Jal, everything started falling apart. No one was prepared for how quickly the universe retracted."

"Now you're after it," Javier said. "You realize that, don't you? That you are after it? The universe is gone, traveler. You're on the life raft of humanity. Human, Cyborg, Finturnian, Necrodian, and every other manner of sentience that could come together is clinging to life here. This planet was built. We designed it so it could pass through the imploding wave and hover in the existence outside."

"That's the Edge of Time for you," Javier continued. "A planet ship that escaped the implosion, that is now more jacked up than any of us could ever hope to fix, ever since the robots turned treacherous and tried to destroy us, that is. Chances are we have less than a decade. That's what the experts say, at least."

Vaks downed his whiskey, and Javier refilled it. "So this is it then?"

Javier nodded and sipped. "It could be worse."

"I suppose so."

"That number is an estimate by the way. It's been speeding up and slowing down lately. I'm beginning to think it's less reliable than we are giving it credit for."

Vaks closed his eyes and sighed.

"It's not so bad though; I think I know where your StoryTeller can be found. I haven't been to Cantor in over a year, but the Governor has been concerned about a religious group that has been sprouting up. At least he was a while ago. I don't know what's happened with it."

"You know the Governor?"

"Well, I've lived here at the border of the desert for a long time, and the Governor and I have a special relationship on some policies that encroach on my rights. He's a reasonable man, though."

"How long will it take to get there?"

"Not more than three days."

Vaks brightened when he heard that.

"By the way," Javier said, filling his third glass of whiskey. "Why are you after this StoryTeller anyway?"

Vaks lowered his eyes and seethed with rage as the memory of answers filled him without warning. He took a deep breath. "Allow me to continue my story, and you will know well enough."

"On one condition."

Vaks raised an eyebrow.

"We take another shot before you start talking."

Vaks could not resist breaking into a cheery grin. This man was speaking his language. It was one of the best parts of StoryTelling. Just about every place he had ever been to had awesome booze lurking somewhere in its culture. Vaks sought it out, and he was often chastised by his Order for doing so.

When the shot was slammed and the glasses refilled, Vaks felt he could continue.

Chapter 6 - The Doctor

Cartin Delgado had never dreamed of being happier. She was now married to the love of her life, someone she had spent much of her childhood playing make believe with, and a man who was also one of the greatest explorers of the entire colony. They told stories about how brave he was in the tunnels, and it made her glow with pride that the man who loved her was such a good man.

Their honeymoon was in a distant cavern, long abandoned; its overhead embedded with glowing blue gemstones. There weren't a lot of miners that even knew about places like that.

They were hard to separate, and on the third day after their marriage they started working in the same mine together. Their request was unanimously approved, and the support that both of them had received from the community expedited the reassignment. They started their first day of work together in a challenging sector of the mine, but not one as dangerous as the exploration mines that Mikhail had transferred from.

Being an explorer, Mikhail was skilled in just about everything a miner could do that was useful, and when the lead drill seized and stopped progress, Mikhail offered to fix it. The others agreed and soon Mikhail was halfway swallowed by the machine, reaching inward to realign the inner cylinders.

Cartin smiled as she watched, but soon found her joy evacuating as a nightmare began to unfold.

The equipment was starting up.

This shouldn't have been possible. The machine was supposed to be de-energized! Steam hissed as the drill began performing the automated system initialization, and Cartin knew that Mikhail had only a few seconds left before the jaw of gears and levers closed on him.

Cartin screamed, thrusting her arm inside to grab the collar of her husband's shirt, but it was too late. The final software had engaged and the fairing slammed shut. The multi-ton equipment clenched its maw of gears with unyielding hydraulic pressure upon them, tearing through flesh, blood, and bone.

Cartin's arm was caught with Mikhail's body in the gears of the machine, whose grinding churned them together into oozing red pulp. There was a screech and then a loud bang, a gurgling exhalation of steam, and all Cartin could hear were her own screams as she writhed on the ground, blood spurting from her gaping arm.

Cartin could hear her parents' voices.

They were talking to the Doctor.

She recognized his voice.

There was only one doctor in the entire colony, and it was his job to serve the population's needs.

She wondered why she couldn't move. The situation felt strange. She could feel the wind against her skin and the soft table underneath her, warm with her body heat. Cartin could also hear everything going on around her, but couldn't move her eyes.

They were talking about the surgery.

"I know it's a dangerous procedure, but it's the only way to save your daughter's life. If we send her to Cantor, she'll die on the journey there. The only hope is a cybernetic fusion."

The words hung in the air like a bitter mist.

"A cybernetic fusion is a very painful process that splices organic nerve tissue with electrical wiring and fuses a cybernetic organism onto the human body. In this case, it is going to be an entire arm. Limbs are said to be the most excruciating," the Doctor explained to Cartin's mother. "Though, they do sometimes afford unique opportunities."

Cartin's mother looked at her daughter, holding a tissue to her nose, her knuckles gripping it tightly. Cartin could only see her as a blur in her peripherals, but she understood what her mother was going to consent for.

"Do it."

"Thank you, Mrs. Delgado."

Cartin panicked, though she was helpless to move a single part of her body to do anything about it; her parents turned and left the room.

"I hope you understand that we had to make the decision for you. You would be too far taken by the pain of your wound to make a rational decision," the Doctor said to Cartin, leaning over her. She was wearing a gown now. She thought about her missing arm and pain seared into her mind. "This is going to sting a bit," the Doctor said as he started slicing away flesh around the gaping wound.

The procedure called for Cartin's complete mental faculties to remain functioning. To enable this to occur, she was administered a stimulant that unequivocally denied the necessary functions of the brain to cease. Because the procedure was excruciatingly painful, however, she was required to be immobilized for the cybernetic growth to take effect.

Through periphery reflected in the stainless-steel furnishing of an overhead light, Cartin watched the scalpel carefully approach her flesh and begin cutting a path for the cybernetic tendrils to enter. The pain was unavoidable, and it pierced her perception, burning forever into her brain.

Over the next several hours, the mythic wires of Cybrint Technology fused with her nervous system and burrowed into her body. It was an excruciating process, and not one that ever guaranteed survival. A Cybrint limb could completely consume a person's sanity and kill them.

When the procedure was done, Cartin lay awake, mentally exhausted but unable to sleep. The pain was gone, and instead she could feel a new sensation where her arm used to be. She still couldn't move, but when she saw the look in the Doctor's eyes as he hovered over her, a bloody face mask covering his mouth and nose, she would have sold her soul to have been able to flee.

"I hope you know this is the only consideration I require as a fee," he said with a sickeningly charming voice.

Cartin heard a zipper unfasten.

"Your family doesn't have the means to pay me, nor does Cantor have the interest in doing so, so I have to take what I can. Consider this the cost of saving your life."

Cartin cried internally, but when she regained her faculties, she was greeted by her parents and refused to talk about what had happened. Stricken with grief, not only from the loss of Mikhail, but also from the horror she had been victim to, Cartin seldom left her room. She cried when she was alone, and snapped hateful comments at her parents, further receding into her dark isolation.

At last, her courage got the better of her, and Cartin rose from her depression and walked to the Doctor's residence in the mine. She tore the door off the entrance with her new robotic arm, the metal hinges ripping like paper. The Doctor was sitting to supper when Cartin arrived, and the remains of his meal went scattering along with the table that she flung across the room.

Cartin held him at her mercy within a matter of seconds. Her cyborg arm was a powerful mechanism of gears with five crushing digits that could grip and shear metal. The skull of a man was as soft as an egg now. Her new arm clenched him tightly, operating in parallel with her human mind as if it had grown naturally out of her shoulder.

"Please don't kill me!" he begged, clutching his hands and quivering.

"It's not going to be now, but *I am going to kill you,*" Cartin hissed. "The *minute* you stop being useful to the colony as a doctor, I am going to tear your esophagus through your stomach." Cartin clenched his throat until his voice creaked involuntarily. "Don't even think about doing what you did again, or I swear on every Story ever told I will make you pay!"

The Doctor's eyes were rolling back into his head. Cartin was fueled with rage, using all her strength to hold off the need to murder the man here and now. She left without saying another word, returned to her home, and cried. When she was exhausted of crying, she read and reread all the letters Mikhail had written to her and fell asleep.

It was less than two months before they had started running out of food and Cantor refused to send in another food supply. The drill that had killed Mikhail and taken Cartin's left arm was destroyed in the process, and Cantor was so furious with the matter that they gave up entirely on the colony and cut off all supply shipments.

Cartin was encouraged by her parents to go with a group of representatives and plead with the Governor about changing his mind and sustaining the colony. She'd give anything to get away from Vastrix since the accident and accepted the mission, the confusion of her rage toward the Doctor and her own survivor's guilt driving her mad.

She needed to run away. To regain her balance somewhere, anywhere away from everything that reminded her of the pain. She needed to use her rage and fury as fuel for a mission, and to return from the Capitol with supplies.

While she was gone she could forget about everything that was wrong back home. She didn't blame her parents for consenting to the procedure for her—she would have consented herself, but she blamed them because they did nothing about what happened to her after.

She had confessed the situation to them one morning, unable to bear it all inside for another minute. They had sympathized with her, knowing she was deeply hurt and struggling to reconcile her pain without pursuing the Doctor's death, but they would not go after him either. They supported her decision to let him live. It drove Cartin crazy. She wasn't sure if she was living in a strange, twisted nightmare where everyone's insanity allowed such a monstrous act to happen, or if this was really the way the world was. She desperately scrambled to be free of it, needing something from the outside to grab onto and pull her away.

This was her chance. A trip to Cantor was just what she needed. She had only ever been to the outskirts of Cantor when she was a small child, too young to work in the mines. She was a girl then, and they rode out together on the Steam Horses and visited the outpost, her father telling her of adventures from his favorite heroes. Cartin hadn't been on a trip like this since she started full-time employment in the mines, but since the accident she still had not returned to work. When the opportunity arose for her father to arrange for Cartin to ride with the team to collect supplies, he did so immediately.

The situation had become dire. It wouldn't be long before they'd start losing the weak to starvation, and that was already with rationed food supplies.

When the mission was approved, and Cartin was given permission to travel, they left immediately. The party climbed aboard their Steam Horses and raced across the Needle highway toward the Wastes. There wasn't much left in the land out here other than scorched graphite, but that which there was to see, rose across the land as obsidian spires of twisted creation, petrified tongues of black earth, super-heated into gleaming stone. Cartin loved the highway out of the mountains because of this, and particularly because of the shapes the sunlight reflected off the shining, black spires.

The Steam Horses were very peculiar creatures. They were former biological organisms that had long ago fused with a similar technology that was a prototype of Cybrint technology. The very same tech that started the cybernetic movement long before the Edge of Time was ever even a thought. The cybernetics enhanced their brains, and, remarkably enough, they had enough consciousness to protect themselves from the A.I. virus when it struck, causing them to be among the few cyborg species to remain alive. They were a descendent of the Earth horse, and were among the few species of animals that had survived from that antediluvian planet.

The Steam Horse had both a sentience that desired, and a compulsion that demanded to be ridden by the will of a rider. Not all Steam Horses were easy to ride with, but when a pair was made, the combined sentience allowed for extraordinary possibilities.

Cartin chose the wildest beast there was, gripping the metallic mane in her own metallic fingers, and holding its torso firmly in the control of her thighs. They rode seamlessly across the land.

Before the others, Cartin reached the place that she had gone as a child, and saw now that it was much different. The great, brilliant outpost with its lasers and electromagnetic shielding was a marvel back then, but now it was a husk of technology, with canvas tarps covering the planes where an electromagnetic field used to be. There was now a single old man that remained stationed.

He saw Cartin race into the plaza, reigning in her Steam Horse at the last minute, sending a plume of dust into the air around her. He had been watching from his perch on the outpost walls with his binoculars. The platform was shaded by a wide pink umbrella, under which he sat with book spread open on his lap. He sighed and rose from his seat, slowly walking down the stairs, carefully breathing in and out. The last thing he wanted to do now was deal with another crazy kid, especially when he had darker matters to deal with. He paused at the hall mirror during his descent from his perch and tucked his uniform neatly in place.

"Can I help you with something ma'am?" The man said, startling Cartin who was sullenly glaring at the ground between her feet, her hands clenched into iron balls.

She looked up at him.

The man was wearing a faded blue uniform with a military insignia on the left breast. He had a weapon holstered at his hip. Cartin wasn't sure what kind of weapon it was since it resembled a revolver. It could have had a gravity mod on it for all Cartin knew.

"Yes, I'm Cartin Delgado, representative of Vastrix mining colony. We are here to petition the Governor for supplies. We are starving up there."

The man never took his eyes off of her. They were kind. His gray eyebrows concernedly pointing down. He nodded to her. "We've received your requests here, and the Governor is informed of your need. We are, however, also in dire times in Cantor and, as such, it is difficult to provide for everyone's need."

It sounded strange, as if he was reciting a script.

"Forgive me," the man said. "I am speaking for the Governor when I say he apologizes for being unable to meet you, but he has dispatched supplies that should sustain you for several more months. By then, the problem of production should be resolved."

"There is nothing to forgive—thank you!" Cartin turned and looked at the other delegates who were now arriving in her wake.

"If you will all please wait here until the supplies arrive, I will send word at once." The man turned around and started walking toward the outpost tower adjacent to his perch, which was precariously built on three posts.

"Sir?" Cartin called after him.

He turned to acknowledge her.

"Can you tell me what your name is, please?"

The man hesitated. "Mr. Talka."

There was a stillness in the air as he said his name, and it hung about them unnaturally long, until an eerie wind came by and carried it away.

Mr. Talka started climbing the thin wooden ladder to the outpost tower, hesitating as it started creaking under his weight, the rickety structure threatening to collapse. He reached the platform and sat in a pink lawn chair after unfolding it. There was a wire connected to a microphone that he talked into that led to a piece of twisted metal at the peak of the polka dot canopy above.

Some good news at last, Cartin thought. They were going to return to Vastrix sooner than anticipated with the supplies. It was reassuring to know that the Governor was not abandoning them. Mr. Talka was gazing out toward the horizon with a set of binoculars as they waited.

This was working out better than Cartin had expected. After some time, the man abruptly straightened and then started climbing down the ladder alarmingly fast. He ran to the operational control panel and opened the outpost gates.

It seemed like a futile gesture since the walls did not extend much further than the gate itself, and yet Cartin could see now, through the open outpost doors, a small band of vehicles racing up from the horizon. They must be carrying quite a few supply trucks with the dust cloud they produced.

Cartin and her team of delegates tensely awaited the arrival of the vehicles. Each of them stayed close to their Steam Horses, whose uneasiness escalated the tension of the situation.

As the vehicles drove closer, Cartin realized that there weren't any supply trucks. All that dust was coming from an arsenal. It dawned on Cartin what was happening, and she screamed at the top of her lungs, "RUUUN!!!"

She swung her legs over the side of her Steam Horse and with an intense desire to escape the approaching terror, they shot into the desert. The other miners were quick to do the same, but it was not before bullets started flying. They were using gravity rounds. None of the miners had access to that kind of technology. They were virtually unarmed against it.

A miner screamed, and there was a shrill neigh as the Steam Horse shattered with the tearing carnage of a gravity round. The bullet tore through metal and flesh, causing its legs to fail and sending the noble beast crashing into the ground, blood and oil spraying up from its remains.

Cartin rode on, gravity rounds racing by her ears, pulling her.

There were more cries as they were each ridden down. Cartin was last alive, her Steam Horse far ahead of the others, threatening the attackers to break free.

She was far on the horizon now, moving faster than their vehicles, moving faster than she'd ever gone before.

The air cracked like a whip and her Steam Horse screamed, throwing Cartin into a turbulent slide across the sand. She crashed into a rock and flipped upward, her metallic fingers scraping the graphite as she clung to whatever was in reach. She crashed hard to a stop, absorbing most of the force into her cybernetic arm.

She gasped for air, the pain in her ribs and legs was so immense that she could barely move. Her Steam Horse was crying out to her from a ruin of flesh and wires, blue blood spraying out of interior tubes. The same color blood that would eventually flow through Cartin's own cybernetic veins.

She remembered the Doctor, and it brought rage into her to think of dying here before she could put him to justice. She straightened her back. Blood spurted from a wet cough as she pushed herself up to her knees.

There was a gunshot, and the Steam Horse was silenced.

Cartin gasped for air between waves of pain as she faced a man with a wolfish grin. He was wearing the black armor of Cantor and had a green circle tattooed on his forehead.

"So this is the last one?"

"Yes, sir."

"*Why!?*" Cartin snarled, clutching her ribs.

The man looked pitifully down at her. "Because your colony has ceased being productive and must be eliminated from the expenditures. Cantor will not replace the drill that miner destroyed with his body, nor will we waste supplies in a project that serves no purpose. We have all the ore that we could possibly need until the planet dies. There is no use for you. It is inconvenient for you that you must die for this to happen, but please rest assured that Cantor has its citizens' best interests at heart."

"*No!*" She spat. "You *will not* kill me!"

The man paused and stared at Cartin for a long time. He was both hypnotized and terrified of the furious beast that glared through the bloody face of her broken body. His gun was aimed at her skull. Cartin's teeth clenched tighter, and the man lowered it.

He nodded to one of the men, and they started leaving.

Cartin was alone in the desert, her body broken from the crash, her very purpose in living taken away, and all she could think about was staying alive long enough to murder the Doctor. She agonizingly picked up her body and was thankful to have no broken limbs to prevent her from walking. She looked at the horizon and knew she had no hope to make it back. She was going to die out here.

Chapter 7 - Loss

"I'm not going to take it anymore, Vaks!" Sheila screamed. "I won't keep living like this!"

"What do you want me to do, Sheila!" Vaks yelled back, a hysterical baby writhing in his arms. There was so much noise in the living room it was driving him insane. It didn't help that Entropy had started hanging out in Astro's room when Vaks went to sleep. He wasn't sure what could be done about it. Hallucinations do what they want. No one noticed Entropy but him, and it was making him more and more tense each day. The shadows now held an actual body that could step out and speak to him.

He was also being hunted. The Cult of Story had grown into a violent and fanatical group. They believed in a concept known as the Final Story. It was an entity that drank on the human lives devoted to it. They would routinely commit ritual suicide to liberate themselves into the cosmos.

It was a very bizarre religion, but it had not completely taken over the planet yet. There were still many families more concerned about farming and living their lives than any nonsense about a great Story in the sky. However, they were a dying breed, and Vaks, Sheila, and their son were among them.

Vaks had been hiding his identity from the rest of Jal. The Cult had been relentlessly sacrificing people in an attempt to usher in an apocalypse. It had truly gotten out of hand to a frightening degree. So much so that people were no longer seen about on roads at night. Seldom were there children wandering about in the forests. These were dark days on Jal, and there were worse dangers that started emerging in the shaded places.

"Here!" Sheila said, exasperated. She took the screaming baby out of Vaks' arms. The baby calmed, and Sheila glared at Vaks. "I want you to do something about it! Make it stop! Use your magic or something and make them stop killing people!"

"That's not the way it works, Sheila. You know that."

"I know that you *should* know, but you're just a kid compared to some of the people at your Order aren't you!"

Vaks felt the sting in silence.

"I'm sorry," Sheila said, lowering her voice to a calmer state. "I know it's not your fault, but I just want to feel like the world is not actually ending."

"I *am* doing something about it, Sheila. I'm doing everything I can! It's not like the world is easy to change. I…don't know what's happening. It's like something fell over the edge."

"Well, maybe you should just leave then." Her words cut deeper than he expected.

Vaks turned without a word and went to retrieve his coat from the rack by the door.

"Where are you going?"

He looked over his shoulder.

"Out."

There was a gasping silence. Then a geyser of lightning. "You're going to go drink again, aren't you?"

"I'm doing something about it, Sheila!"

"Fine! Just go ahead and leave, you jerk! GET OUT!" She

grabbed the ceramic statue of the Buddha and hurled it at him. It crashed against the wall where Vaks' head had been a hair ago. Pieces of ceramic crumbled to the floor.

Vaks looked at it, finished wrapping his scarf around his neck, and before stepping out into the night, turned his head toward Sheila and said, "Clean up this mess."

The door slammed behind him.

His feet crunched through the snow as he tramped toward the orange glow of the town. The cold air felt good against his heat. Sheila opened the door behind him. He could hear the shrieking child as she screamed obscenities at him. He didn't turn around.

The bar waited for him as it usually did, which was much more somber than it had ever been since he had first come across it. Vaks had been coming to this place for over a year. It had once been a place where his closest associates, the ones who knew who he was, could meet him.

They were organizing a secret rebellion and Vaks had provided them essays denouncing the Cult of Story's methods and fanaticism. They didn't even have an effect. They tortured and converted the entire nation at such an alarming rate that the majority ruled tyranically. The rebellion was dwindling fast, and it was a rare moment if Vaks saw someone he recognized besides the owner.

It was quiet and morose. Vaks sat down at the counter and a man who should have been Gart Frankson, the owner, was some rough-looking character Vaks had never seen before. The man was missing a front tooth and had an uncomfortable wickedness in his smile.

"What you drinking?"

"Where's Gart?"

They stared at each other.

"His wife was taken for questioning down at the headquarters.

He followed her and is protesting the Prime Priest now. I was sent to fill in during his absence."

Vaks narrowed his eyes. "Oh. Give me an ale then."

"Which family?"

"House."

Vaks took a sip of his drink and felt relieved. He shifted his attention to the rest of the room. The bartender was not moving away. He looked at him uncomfortably standing there, wanting payment. Vaks pulled out his wallet.

"No, no," he said, waving away the money. "This one is on the house."

There was a frightening gleam in his eye. Cruelty in his grin.

Vaks stood up abruptly, nearly spilling his ale. From the darkness he heard Entropy's rasping laugh like a gurgling rhythm to the discord of evil. The bartender laughed as Vaks burst out of the building, running home. Something strange was happening. Everything was out of the ordinary. The windows were closed, the blinds shutting off from the world their internal glow. Vaks ran back home, thinking only of his wife and son.

He had been waiting to hear about arrangements to leave the planet. It was his emergency plan. To go as stowaways on a shuttle and then once they got safely settled somewhere, he'd go back to the Halls of Remembrance. Until then, he'd just have to hope that they didn't come hunting for him. It wouldn't be long before they did.

There was something strange going on tonight and Vaks knew it. He reached the slope up toward his house and saw at least five pairs of foot prints leading up through the snow toward his doorstep.

Vaks sprinted up the hill.

The door was ajar, and he crashed through it, only to get slammed in the chest and thrown backwards. Vaks went doubling over with a cry of pain. He forced his face upward, reigning tightly in on his concentration. There were men with crossbows to his right and left, their sights trained on him.

An iron club was aimed lethally at Vaks' head. The man holding it was grinning savagely.

In the center of the room, Sheila had a knife to her throat. She was straining her head back from the edge pressing into her skin, the man holding her hostage smiling with macabre pleasure.

A man in a black robe walked out from the kitchen holding their child. Sheila burst into tears. The child was calm and playful in the man's arms as he waggled a finger over him.

"Let them go…" Vaks growled, recovering his breath.

The man smirked and casually tossed the baby to Sheila, who was released by her captor to catch the child, which she did with a cry and whimper, thankful to have not dropped him. Sheila fell to her knees and wept over her young son.

"You know we just need your blood. All of it in fact. It's just the kind of stuff that makes these rituals really…pop." The man who had thrown his child told Vaks.

"Get out of my home," Vaks growled again.

"Seriously, Vaks, get on my level. We are going to cut open your arteries and nail you to a star. It's all going to collect in a pool so we can properly pay homage."

"What's wrong with you!?"

"Not me! No, no, no! I'm perfectly normal, yessiree. We just want to summon the end, that's all. There's a lot of angry evil in this universe that's been thwarted for too long." He placed his hands on his hips and looked affectionately over the child. "I didn't know you have a son."

"Keep your hands off him!" Vaks thrust himself forward, but a boot collided with his ribs and sent him tumbling to the side.

"I'll go willingly!" Vaks said through gritted teeth. "Just let

Sheila and the child go!"

"Oh, Sheila is no matter of ours. She's a right floozy though I see." He leered over her body. "I'm looking forward to getting to know her better."

"Stay away from us!"

"Look, Vaks, you are in no position to make demands, so just sit your tight little petootie down. I'm going to bludgeon you within an inch of your life, then I am going to violate you beyond your worst nightmares, and when we arrive in the city, you will be crucified. There your son will be devoured in a ceremonial ritual feast, as we do with all the children who are chosen! It is a pleasant surprise considering the occasion." He wiped dribble from his lips. "You should feel honored, really. Your death is an essential part of the awakening."

"Just let me say goodbye to my son," Vaks threw every bit of his mental strength at the man, knowing he was at his mercy. With the gift of StoryTelling, he put the weight of fatherhood in the subtext of his words and forced it into their minds with the trained ability of those of his order. He created the empathy he needed.

"Very well," the man smirked and snatched the child roughly from Sheila's arms, carrying him over to Vaks. She burst into tears again. The other assassins that were keeping Vaks and Sheila subdued stood nearby, their eyes shifting uneasily. Their leader should not have been acting like this. Vaks knew he would not be able to keep up the ruse for long.

Sheila whimpered and made eye contact with Vaks, but he paid close attention to his son when he was delivered back to him. The man orchestrating this nightmare laughed with delight.

His son was lain on the ground before him. Vaks had been clutching his fist over his chest in prayer as this happened, and detached the small glass vial that hung around his neck.

This was their only chance. He had to hope that they would be merciful to Sheila, and as he thought of his options for salvation, his stomach turned.

He could fight, but they would kill Sheila. Vaks was outnumbered by more than what he could fight alone. They would kill him. The risks of the Sands of Time were great as well. Vaks would survive, in fact much of the universe would be righted by him going back to the Halls of Remembrance, but it was his son that was the concern. The Sands of Time killed roughly one tenth of every subject ingesting them for the first time. Candidates were chosen specifically, and most of them were written off as natural attrition involved in the making of StoryTellers.

The Sands of Time were the substance that allowed the StoryTellers to walk between dimensions of space and time. They were what opened up the channels of the brain to access the secrets of consciousness. They were his return ticket home.

Vaks let his emotions wash over him, his tears filling up his eyes. Even as he was making his decision, he hated what he was doing. It was wrong; it was painful; it was leaving Sheila to the mercy of evil men. He had to save his son though. He could not let his son be devoured by lunatic cultists. Even if he died in the escape.

Vaks crushed the vial surreptitiously in his fist, and brought his hands to his lips, mumbling prayers of thanks as a distraction. The child was a mess of tears and running snot. Vaks felt the grains of sand and crushed glass attach to his tongue, mingling with the blood of his split lip. It took only one grain of Sand to return home, and there was more than enough for two.

He gambled a look at Sheila, whose eyes were gleaming with fear and apprehension. She knew what he was doing. He had talked about it before. Had talked about how once he swallowed the Sands of Time, he would be going home. Her eyes were wild with panic as she placed the pieces of what he was going to do together in her mind.

He was leaving her.

Vaks made eye contact with Sheila for the final time and transmitted everything he could about love and regret, and the promises of coming back to her, but there was no shaking the undercurrent of betrayal and dread.

The sand and blood had mixed, and when Vaks leaned over his son to comfort his crying, he allowed a fraction of Sands to pass from his lips to his son's. It was only a matter of seconds now. He watched his son's throat spasm as he swallowed the sand, and Vaks too consumed what remained of the vial.

The next instant they were removed from Jal and racing through the infinite smallness of space-time until they had both appeared at the Halls of Remembrance.

The boy cried out in anguish. It was a terribly traumatizing experience traveling through the Sands of Time at first, and his son was no exception to the fact. Despite his wails, Vaks felt a surge of exuberance! He had survived the jump! True, it meant he was saved from the evils of Jal, but it also meant that he was now destined to become a StoryTeller.

He felt a stab of pain shoot through his mind as the immense pride he felt for his son and the immense shame he felt for leaving his wife collided.

Vaks scooped up his son and sprinted through the stone courtyard, running past the apprentices and veteran Tellers. He ignored the hails by leaders and proceeded directly to the nursery where he thrust his child into the caring arms of one of the servants.

"This is my son. Please care for him!" That was all Vaks said in his breathlessness before turning about and sprinting out of the nursery, leaving the cries of his child forever haunting the halls behind him.

Vaks crashed through a passageway, shoving a group of Story-Tellers out of the way.

One of them reacted aggressively and whipped an arm out to grab Vaks.

"Watch where you are going, punk!" The older man said, his hand like a vice on Vaks' wrist.

Vaks lashed his right hand out and chopped at the wrist restraining him. The hold broke from Vaks' strike, causing the man to recoil. Before his friends could respond, Vaks was already sprinting down the hallway toward the Pools of Memory where the Sands of Time were stored.

There were calculations to determine how much time was passing on different worlds while one was at the Halls of Remembrance, but it was a convoluted calculation that was relative to each planet, and a terrible chore to figure out, so Vaks operated on a simple, logical course of action: Move as fast as humanly possible.

It could be weeks later on Jal after just an hour at the Halls of Remembrance. The Elders were startled by his abrupt entrance into the chamber, but Vaks did not stop his movement to explain his intrusion.

He had to explain as he worked. It was tough business calculating the required grains of Sand so quickly, but it had to be done. He stood at the workshop mixing and weighing the required sample as he let a torrent of explanation spill from his mouth.

The Elders, in their wisdom, accepted his urgency at face value, and despite his unconventional means of liberating the Sands that he needed, they listened to his reasons. There was much a StoryTeller could know about a person by simply observing. The Elders understood Vaks more than anyone after training him throughout his life.

He prepared his return to Jal unimpeded by the Order. He hadn't been at the Halls of Remembrance for more than an hour by the time he was ready to return. One of the Elders stepped close and put a gentle hand on Vaks' shoulder.

"Before you go, Vaks, it is evident that this is the result of Entropy's awakening. There have been strange occurrences throughout the universe, and many StoryTellers are returning with Memories that seem to contradict the Great Story of the human race. We have known you well enough to trust this emergency to which you are responding, Vaks. We will tend to your son here and teach him the ways. Until then, go and resolve that which you must on Jal, but be careful, Entropy is afoot in the cosmos."

Vaks held the man's gaze. The gravity of his situation was wearing creases into his skin. There was a sickening sensation as he realized that Entropy had not come with him from Jal. It had always been hiding in his shadow. He shuddered at the prospect of Entropy remaining behind, whispering seeds of evil.

Sheila was still there.

"Thank you," Vaks said, and swallowed the new mixture of Sand. He had not been back to the Halls of Remembrance in years, and now, after such a long time shirking his duty as a StoryTeller, he returned only to leave again within the hour. Life was on the line after all. As he swallowed down the gritty solution, he felt the vacuum on his soul and he transported across time and space once more.

Chapter 8 - The Halls of Remembrance

Javier leaned back in his chair and whistled. "What was Jal like when you got back?"

Vaks gave him a tortured look. "Why don't you tell me?"

"You mean, about what happened to the planet years later?"

Vaks nodded.

"I guess you wouldn't have known how it ended up after all. I've only seen the historical account of the planet, though. Just a list of photographs and a habitation rating of one for 'intolerant to life'." There have been a number of ghost stories themed about the planet, but nothing that survives today as real data."

"What have you seen about the planet?"

Javier sighed uneasily and stood up, straightening himself on the edge of the table. "I'm going to crack open another bottle of booze."

As Javier made his way back to the cabinet, Vaks took a deep breath. He needed a minute to relax his mind. It was not easy reliving this. He tried to leave out as much of Entropy as he could. He wasn't sure how comfortable Javier would be knowing Vaks was living in a state of precarious insanity.

"Jal had ceased communication for a number of years, and after not responding to a series of hails from the Galactic Architecture, a vessel was sent to explore what happened." Javier plopped down in his seat uneasily and refilled their glasses. "Readings from the atmosphere showed the planet was habitable by all atmospheric conditions and parameters, but it did not contain any traces of human life at all."

Vaks took a sip. "Did they land on the planet?"

Javier nodded.

"And?"

"Dead. All of them. But...not in ordinary ways. They were perversely killed. The entire planet. It's as if everyone had decided on a certain day that it was the day to die, and they helped each other make it happen. There were piles of corpses in the streets, crucifixions, and strange ritual dismemberments. There were some images that showed things that seemed impossible to explain, like bodies that had been torn apart, with searing burns on their skin where a clawed hand grabbed them." He flexed his fingers out dramatically.

"I see how it might have ended up like that."

"But why did they even let you go back? I mean, you had been shirking your duty there, hadn't you? You were breaking the rules and telling stories all that time. Why did they even permit it?"

"The Elders of the Halls of Remembrance are wise, and even though there are rules and laws that we must follow, they are always held up for interpretation in special circumstances. I was going to go whether they allowed me or not. They knew this and made the best of it."

"And so you went back to save Sheila, right? But you weren't sure if you'd make it in time?"

Vaks nodded.

"I don't want to know what happened, do I?"

"That's up to you. You know how the planet ended up. You

already know what happened."

"But not about what happened to you. Was Sheila there when everyone died?"

Vaks remained silent.

"Look, how about we change the subject?" Javier suggested.

"I failed, alright!?" Vaks snapped, slapping his hands on the table, startling Javier. "I don't know what I was thinking at the time. I should have known that too much time would pass." He hung his head down in shame.

"It was too late then?"

"By several years."

They paused and their whiskey glasses sat untouched on the table.

"She thought I abandoned her."

"She might have thought you saved her son."

"No. When I got back, it was already over. The village I had lived near had been burnt to cinders. The bodies of the townsfolk were charred skeletons nailed upside-down on pentacle crucifixes. The people that I did come across on the way to the city were feral and savage, more beast than human."

"When I made it to the city, I learned that the Cult of Story had consumed the entire nation and imposed its insanity on every man, woman, and child. They had seemed to lose their minds, driven only by pain, fear, and blood. The whole purpose of their religion was to use the blood of StoryTellers in some bizarre summoning ritual."

"Hmmmm," Javier said, scratching his chin musingly.

Vaks scoffed. "My own wife became the High Priest's concubine and was the woman for every depraved ritual the High Priest performed with the rest of its leaders." Vaks clenched his fist and glared at the floor before continuing. "I saw the photos in their newspaper. My own wife, the center of some sick orgy, laughing in the gore of it."

Javier paled.

"I never found her. I did learn that she had confessed herself to the High Priest and became his slave within the week of my departure though. She was venerated as a holy woman for carrying the seed of a StoryTeller inside of her." Vaks growled with frustration and slammed his hand on the table again. "A week! She gave up on me after a week!"

"Well…how long would you have gone?"

"That is beside the point. She might have run, or fought, or… done something! No, instead she got swept right up in the evil of it all."

"Vaks," Javier said with a stern voice. "She didn't have much choice. She was being held hostage. She was already captured."

"Yeah, but…"

"There was something bigger happening on Jal than just stories and romance, Vaks." Javier let a pause hang between them. "Something happened that exceeded the individuals involved. Don't give me that look either, I'm not a follower of the Story."

Vaks thought of the grin on Entropy's face as he whispered into the people's ears while Vaks was telling Stories. They had clapped along and laughed joyously, while Vaks wondered what discordant evils were being seeded into their consciousness.

"Jal was not the start of Entropy."

"What makes you say that?" Javier asked, puzzled.

"They were just an illusion of some greater force acting in the cosmos."

"Like what?"

"Like what Entropy really is."

Javier raised an eyebrow. "The undoing force that destroys, right? That is what we are talking about here? The one that collapsed all the particles and energy of the universe into itself, effectively destroying it all or dumping it into another dimension, both of which are irrelevant to life now? That Entropy?"

Vaks looked at him quietly for a long time, the darkness in his eyes deepening. Entropy was sliding its lanky body from a crevice above the ajar closet door. It slithered against the walls, a human snake until it was hovering silently behind Javier.

"Vaks!" Javier cried out, leaning back in his seat.

Vaks shook his head, and Entropy was gone. It was lurking back in the dark corners of the room, silently grinning its masquerade smile.

"Yes, that is the Entropy we are talking about."

Javier shuddered. "It gives me spiders just thinking about it. That whole planet is a frightening mystery. Evils happened there that never *were*, and never *will be*, explained. There were some very strange forces at work there, and what kind of evidence was found to have come out of the ground there defies reason." Javier sighed. "It's been bad here too though, and I mean *really* bad, just not as bad as Jal."

"What do you mean?"

"About Jal, or here?"

"Forget Jal."

There was a stiff silence before Javier continued.

"The land was irradiated in many places after the A.I. sabotage. Most of the planet was killed, the animals with it. There were some species that mutated, however. It seems they keep getting worse and worse too."

A weighty silence hung in the air.

"Tell me something, Vaks."

"What's that?"

There was a terrible sadness in Javier's eyes as he looked at him. They bore a knowledge and wisdom that Vaks hadn't noticed before. His mustache twitched and his eyes lightened softly. "Tell me a story, Vaks. Tell me a story of when you were happy."

He held up a hand to stop Vaks from speaking.

"No! Before we take this tale any further, while you are closest to the energy that draws power to you, I must say this…" His visage was appearing hazy to Vaks' increasing drunkenness. "Do not drown in the vengeance before you breathe a memory of joy. If you tell me the reason why you look as grim as you do—because I don't believe it's Sheila—you may not be able to remember anything happy again."

"That's bullshit, you know."

"What?"

"That I won't still remember it."

"What do you mean?"

"I'm a StoryTeller," Vaks shrugged. "I remember stories. Especially the happy ones."

Chapter 9 - Metal Knuckles

Cartin was found by a scavenging party that was out exploring ruins for resources the city could use. It was a dangerous living, but it certainly paid. Most of the scavengers were extremely wealthy, but without the technological resources, or the know how to reinvent them, humanity was resorting to creatively employing an arsenal of increasingly primitive innovations.

Cartin was stretched out across the sand, crawling to her last moments of consciousness. Her metal fingers reaching outward for life, frozen in air.

A boy jumped from the scavenge wagon and landed lightly on his toes, bursting into a sprint toward Cartin's body.

The scavenge wagon slowed to a stop.

The boy called out to the huge machine.

Banging came from inside the door and it slid open. An angry old man peered his disheveled, balding head out and spotted the boy. He frowned and stepped outside. He was wearing brown overalls and a dust-yellowed shirt. He leapt spryly from the scavenge wagon and stood next to the boy scratching his head.

As they were pondering Cartin's young cyborg corpse, she stirred.

The old man swatted the boy's shoulder and barked at him,

pointing at the wagon.

The boy darted inside.

The old man gently turned Cartin over and laid her face up.

Cartin's chest rose with a gentle breath and her eyes cracked open enough for her to recognize the shape of a human being providing help. She passed out.

When Cartin awoke she was laying on a plushy cushion in a person-sized metal bin. Half surprised to be alive, she remembered seeing someone giving her help and looked around the room. It was more of a cluttered garage than anything else.

There wasn't anyone she could see at the moment. Maybe they wouldn't know she was awake.

Cartin eased her foot over the side of the bin as carefully as she could.

A young boy walked into the room from a passageway. He stared at Cartin with saucer eyes. Gasping, he bolted away, his feet pattering on the metal grating.

Cartin cursed and dropped down onto the metal. Her legs were weak, and she nearly fell. She held onto an edge for support, her knees shaking. She took a deep breath, steadied herself, and stood up.

The boy came running out, skidding to a stop. An old man wearing brown overalls came walking out and looked suspiciously at Cartin.

"Hello?" Cartin offered. No one spoke. "Thank you for helping me." She offered again.

"He can't speak," the boy said. "His tongue was cut out by mutants a long time ago."

The old man held his face tightly shut in a wrinkled grimace.

"Oh. I'm sorry. What's your name, little boy? My name is Cartin Delgado."

"Freddy. That's Grumps."

The man hit the child firmly across the head. Cartin was startled by the severity, but the boy laughed as if this was their normal interaction with each other.

"Grumpturts is his real name. It is really important to him," the boy explained. "It's just awful to say though. 'Grumpturts.' See what I mean?"

Cartin stared at him blankly. The corner of her mouth twitched, but not enough to make her smile away the bitter thoughts.

"Nice to meet you, Grumpturts. You too, Freddy," Cartin said, the boy failing to suppress a smile as Cartin said the old man's name. Cartin was mortified when she found she could barely control her mouth any longer, having great difficulty holding back a smile.

"Thank you for helping me. Will you please tell me where we are? I need to go back to my family in Vastrix."

Freddy looked up at Grumpturts, his eyes heavy with sorrow.

Grumpturts placed a hand on Freddy's shoulder, and the boy relaxed. His own eyes were blue nebulas buried in the wrinkles of a hard life. She didn't even need to hear the words to know what happened.

As the light struck the intersecting lines of his iris, she felt her heart sink as though it were disappearing into black holes within those nebulas.

Cartin gasped and fell to her knees. The gathered strength from before failing her as her wounded body gave out.

Three days later, Cartin left Grumpturts and Freddy to scavenging. They returned to Vastrix beforehand, and Cartin limped around the crypt that was her home. There had been no mercy. It was a pitiless slaughter; an utter annihilation with no regard for children.

Still, Cartin made her way across the courtyard and the well, looking for survivors. She held onto the pine railing as she climbed the cliffs path to the Heights, supporting her body on the notched wood. When she reached the Heights, it was not long before she was at the Doctor's house. The door was ajar.

Her metal arm pushed it open, shoving aside a pile of debris from an explosion on the other side of the home. Cartin made her way across the piled bricks and reached the entrance to the Doctor's study. It had been taken off its hinges by force.

She stepped inside and disturbed a pile of rubble. The buzzing of flies erupted and black pellets swarmed her.

Cartin screamed, backing away as a mass of flies were disturbed from inside the room and took to the air.

They darkened the light. There were so many. As they filled the room with buzzing, Cartin pulled out the emergency kit she insisted on bringing. Inside were flares. She lit one and threw it into the room. The smoke and light agitated the bugs so much they evacuated the home and disappeared into the sky. What was left was the stench of what had attracted them.

Cartin entered the room again. The flare splashed a quivering red over the walls. She had to cover her nose from the smell. The Doctor's bullet ridden corpse was infested with a writhing mass of maggots. She knew it was the Doctor because of the coat, but also because of the piece of flesh that had ejected from his head. It was just a piece, but it was a miraculously preserved eyeball clinging to a piece of meat on a pile of bricks.

She spat a heavy glob of mucus on the body and left the place. The assault squad that had attacked her had gone on to kill the entire colony. They should have just killed her when they had the chance. She never even got to kill the Doctor herself.

Cartin Delgado did not spend long lamenting, however. Instead, she felt a strange new awakening in the world, much more than that which she had thought possible, and was not prepared for the excitement it inspired. She wasn't going to be a miner anymore, not that she could anyway. What would she do, mine rocks up here in the mountains alone?

As Cartin climbed back aboard the scavenge wagon, she breathed out a sigh of relief. She knew there would be grief. She knew that the grief would come in waves and would consume her entirely. But now, she felt that there was nothing to stop her from killing the ones who killed her people. That freedom, was her life-blood.

By the third day, Cartin had demonstrated a remarkable healing rate, undoubtedly from the successful cyborgian fusion, and was soon taken to the CrossWays where the traders met. Grumpturts allowed Freddy to spend whatever sum of money he wanted on Cartin to prepare her for a life in the world.

Though loss was a heavy anchor in her heart, Cartin allowed the boy to buy her a sturdy traveler's garb and provisions. She even gave him a kiss on the cheek when she boarded the train to Cantor and said goodbye, leaving him in blushing awe.

In addition to the ticket they had bought for her, they had given her a small amount of starting cash to survive on. When Cartin said goodbye to Grumpturts he reminded her of someone so very close and important to her that she might have known him her entire life. She could not remember the name, and wondered who it might have been he reminded her of.

Cartin Delgado knew she would never see Grumpturts and Freddy again. However, their kindness and compassion provided what she needed to prevent her bitterness toward the world from being all consuming.

The cybernetic limb started growing through the rest of her body, and soon she was a complete cyborg. Her organs gradually fused with metallic fibers that clung to her vertebra, stretching through her body. Her life span became dependent on the supplements of Blue Blood the government provided for her kind.

As Cartin looked out the window over the wasted plains of desolation, she wondered what kind of sentience would let such a thing happen. Then she remembered the history of how humans had frequently destroyed entire planets in the span of a few years from irrevocably depleting vital resources. They didn't realize then that they were exterminating an entire piece of the puzzle.

Those were the old days though. The times of light, before the universe ended.

"*Estimated time until arrival in Cantor: Thirty-six minutes,*" a voice boomed over the intercom of the train.

Cartin took a long, deep breath and closed her eyes. When she opened them, she was ready for the rest of her life.

Chapter 10 - Sabotage Love

"YOUCH!" Vaks yelled, grasping for his crotch as he manifested in the air on his first Story.

He hadn't ever used the Sands of Time before. Everything had been theory and concept, doing endless calculations of grain constituent and quantity for use. Vaks was never very good at it. That's not to say that he didn't have the capacity for it. It came to him quite easily, but he just didn't make the effort to learn it as much as the other students did.

He was okay with low performance scores if they were acceptable, and he didn't have to study for them. He just wanted to learn the histories anyway. The stories, the myths, the great memories of the most important StoryTellers of all time. They were his favorite memories to explore. They were the most pivotal moments in humanity, captured in a totally immersive experience. That was where Vaks dwelt when he wasn't chasing girls that is.

It was partly what made him so fixated on the literature of long ago, employing the tales of passionate and compelling romance in his own schemes. Vaks was repeatedly being reprimanded for luring girls into dark corners and seducing them. He never felt guilty about it, though. They certainly instilled a fear of God in him, especially when they flogged him for his attempt to seduce the librarian to gain access to the Elder's library.

"Stop being such a baby," Miranda said, stepping lightly out of the air and onto the grass.

"It feels like my anus was turned inside out," Vaks moaned.

"I remember my first Story," Miranda said with a grin.

Vaks looked up at her and straightened his back. "You know some girls wouldn't brag about that."

She socked him in the arm. "You know, I ought to *actually* turn your anus inside out and see how you like it for a comment like that."

"Seriously though, did it feel like that for you?"

"Yeah."

"Does it get better?"

"Not that I've seen."

"How many Stories have you done so far?"

"You really don't pay attention to things, do you?"

"Look, I was too busy admiring the scenery. Give me a break."

She gave him a sideways glance. "What do you mean?"

"I mean I had other things on my mind. That's all."

She frowned. "Well, this is my fourth."

"Fourth…why would they…"

"Send a four timer on a story with a newbie?" She shrugged. "Who knows? I guess our profiles matched for what they needed."

"You really believe that they always pick the right person for the right Story, or is it only right because the Elders say so?"

"You mean, do I actually believe that fairy tale bologna about the Great Story? That each and every StoryTeller has a specific purpose in weaving the pattern of history's unfolding? Nah. I don't believe a word of that. That's just the Elders keeping themselves in charge."

"Why do you think they held me back then?" Vaks tried to

sound as objective as he could about himself, but he couldn't hide the bitter sting of having to wait as long as he did for his first Story.

"Personally?"

"I'm not talking to a robot."

Miranda rolled her eyes. "Oh, I forgot I was talking to a child who hasn't yet seen the way the universe works."

"Oh, come on, Miranda, seriously? Why did I have to wait so long do you think?"

"How should I know?"

"Because you're their favorite! You have the highest marks, have already been on three successful Stories, and you *know* what it is that the Elders want."

"Well, I wouldn't give me as much credit as that," Miranda said. "But it probably has to do with how romantic you get."

"How does that have anything to do with it!?" Vaks cried out indignantly.

"Look, it's nowhere near my realm of knowledge to support that claim, but from what I understand, romanticism is the most volatile quality a StoryTeller can have, and it endangers them greatly with Interference."

"Come on, I know the rules. I know Interference directly is a crime, but..." He made an unintelligible sound of frustration. "Just because I like reading about love stories does not mean that I am going to screw up StoryTelling!"

"Vaks," Miranda sighed, "let's not have this discussion. I don't know why you had to wait so long, and quite frankly, I am less interested in that as in why they had to choose *me* to chaperone you!"

"Oh, you've got to be kidding me," Vaks rolled his eyes.

"Give it a rest, Vaks," Miranda said, turning away from him and walking toward the town in the distance. "We've got a Story to collect. Let's get this done and you can ask all the questions you want about why when we get back to the Halls."

Vaks ran several paces to catch up with her. "Easy for you to say."

"Focus, Vaks, it's an easy Story, but it's an important one. Surely you paid attention to that part of our briefing, right?"

Vaks nodded. "I'm not completely incompetent."

"Right, but I want to make sure you understand that we have to be at the Fend Cup for the final championship. These moments need a StoryTeller present to capture their memory. I don't know why they chose you for this story," Miranda sighed, "considering how important this is for the human race."

Vaks grinned foolishly. "Probably because they knew I'd be the best at it. After all, I just have to go watch a world championship and have a good time, right? What could even go wrong?"

Vaks realized those words would come to haunt him as he soon as he uttered them. He tried not to dwell on the thought, as theirs was a special mission, and must be enjoyed. They were sent to watch the Fend Cup, which was a worldwide sport where heroic contestants traversed a ludicrously dangerous course for a timed score. The contestant with the lowest time takes home a trophy and an absurd amount of prize money for the nation they represent.

Fend was in fact one of Vaks' most studied topics. It was a remarkable tournament that celebrated the greatest heroes of the land. They would have to fight beasts, leap through traps, and deal with whatever new obstacles the convention could throw at the people. It was a very simple game really, but sounded like a thrill to watch.

Vaks had only read about it in the accounts of the StoryTeller who had come to this planet before, but who had died generations before they chose Vaks for this mission. Vaks envisioned life much like a game of Fend. One had to race down the course, employing whatever arsenal of skills in possession, and face the unexpected and terrifying evils of the world. It was a fight to an unmeasurable but surmountable goal, pitting one against any conceivable threat to survival, and rewarding richly the victors whose individual creativity and courage triumphed over the staggering odds.

The winner of this Fend Cup was a desperate underdog from a poor nation who had never won a championship before. The Story is that she'll win and bring the riches back to her country and start a movement that will eventually lead into a period of global unification and world peace. It was a significant event to watch, and was going to be vital to the collection of memories in the Halls relating to athleticism and humanity.

The success of world peace and cooperation here is the first time in the universe that it will happen as a direct result of sportsmanship. That's why the Elders sent a chaperone for Vaks. Vaks knew that even though he was the right StoryTeller for this mission, he was so new that he couldn't be trusted entirely not to somehow botch the entire thing.

So here he was with Miranda, the star pupil. The StoryTeller who was on a fast track to the higher planes of consciousness. Miranda not only had some of the keenest instincts for the truth, but she was proficient in virtually every skill they taught her. She was ranked higher than Vaks in everything except martial arts.

This was not because she wasn't exceptional at it, but because Vaks was something of an anomaly. He took to martial arts more than anything else and had even stoked a feud between Miranda by repeatedly defeating her in sparring contests.

She was among the best fighters there too. There was something about the way that she struck Vaks that seemed to make her want to hit him again.

They made it inside the city, and Vaks watched as Miranda handled the transaction with the inn owner, claiming their room for the night. The event was tomorrow morning and tonight was an important opportunity to catch a Side-Story.

The celebration and partying before the Fend Cup was a legendary event. Human beings normally could not grasp the scope of relativity the same way that a StoryTeller could, but if they could, they would see that throughout the thousands of colonized planets in the universe, the Fend Cup festivities were often regarded as the most celebratory affair of all timelines.

Vaks was giddy with excitement. He had been all day. This was really the lottery mission. For him, at least. All Vaks had to do was party and watch the greatest sporting event of all time!

When they had situated in their lodgings for the night, having arranged travel to the Fend Cup in the morning, Vaks frantically paced around the room, Miranda patiently reading.

"Come on, Miranda! Close that damned book and grab ahold of my arm. We are gonna go see the night!"

"I have no intention of partying tonight," Miranda said stiffly, not looking up from her book.

Vaks walked over and deftly snatched it from her hands and leapt back. "Don't even pretend like *you*, little miss rockstar StoryTeller, are going to pass up on the extra objective because you are too much of a sourpuss."

Miranda glared at him, leaping from her seat to strangle Vaks. He laughed and leapt away from her hands.

Shocked at her own outrage, Miranda straightened her skirt and lifted her head. She looked condescendingly at Vaks. "Fine, you may escort me tonight around the festivities." She extended her elbow out, and Vaks whooped, linking his arm around hers and pulling her through the front door.

The night was alive with traces of music and celebration. A glow of neon and good cheer hovered above the city beneath the night, the cool, clean air allaying their anxieties.

"When's the last time you got drunk?"

"Excuse me?"

"What? Did I offend you or something?"

"It's a rude question, isn't it?"

Vaks raised an eyebrow. "I didn't think so."

"Not all of us poison our bodies for pleasure you know. I've never been drunk."

Vaks' eyes widened. "What!"

"It's not that unusual!" Miranda objected. "Look, not all of us are rebels like you."

Vaks looked taken aback, pleasantly surprised by the comment. "Rebel?"

"Oh, please. Stop smirking at me."

Vaks ran to get in front of her as they made their way down the paved side streets of the big city, stopping in her path. "Oh, and what is it that makes me such a rebel?"

"You have no regard for the rules, you drink excessively, and you are always chasing girls, leading them away from the Story! I remember when we all had to listen to that horrible lecture about alcohol when you broke into the wine closet and nearly drank yourself to death."

"It was one hell of a night too, I do recall," Vaks said. "I wasn't alone either, you know."

"Ugh, don't even get me started on that floozie!"

"You shouldn't be so judgmental about people, Miranda," Vaks said, his voice dropping an octave below his normal aloof tone, drawing in a new gravitas. "Those are the human qualities we continually preserve."

"Those are the qualities we continually combat."

Vaks started laughing. "Miranda, you know I don't have to explain to you how important a new experience is to a StoryTeller. Even the Elders say that it is important to be aware of alcohol's effects on reality."

Miranda rolled her eyes and sighed. "Fine. You're right, I know. I just don't like it. I've spent my entire life avoiding these kind of bad habits, but I know how important they are to the Story."

"That's what I'm talking about!" Vaks exclaimed, grabbing her hand and pulling her along the street in a run.

Warmth and electricity coursed through their fingertips as they raced down the metropolis toward the first tavern Vaks could find. There were throngs of people milling about the streets as they approached the festivities. Fireworks blasted in the air and music saturated the night. It was a marvelous display of human abandonment. Even Miranda was being converted to the moment by the awe of such felicity.

When he slowed to a stop, Miranda's grumpiness had melted into joy. Her cheeks were flushed from running, but it appeared to Vaks as though she were beginning to come around.

They were here to have a good time, and they both realized it. That was the beauty of the universe, it seemed to Vaks. Sometimes, the most important cosmic act is to simply enjoy the treasure of being a lowly human.

Chapter 11 - Love and Promises

"You mean to tell me that you actually attended one of the Fend Cups?" Javier said, astonished.

Vaks nodded, a smile hiding behind his face.

Javier threw his hands in the air. "Agh!!! I would give anything to have seen one of those events!"

"Well...we never actually saw the championship," Vaks confessed.

"What do you mean?"

"We...um...got tangled up."

Javier blinked back. "You...got tangled up?"

Vaks nodded and couldn't prevent the redness from coming to his cheeks. Perhaps Javier would attribute it to the alcohol.

"Wait a minute," Javier said, pointing a wobbling finger at Vaks. "You have to give me the details of what happened."

Vaks bellowed with laughter, slamming his hand on the table. Whiskey spilled over from a half empty glass and neither of them paid attention to it. "I'm not going to give you every detail! That is none of your business."

"At least tell me what happened!"

"Well, it's not as happy as you think," Vaks said. "That night we wound up drinking and celebrating in the full spirit of the event, and it wasn't long before we were both drunk, in each other's arms, and whispering our deepest desires for one another."

"Go on," Javier said, and Vaks gave him an irritable look.

"The next morning we woke in the same bed together."

"Did you…" Javier was clutching the edge of the table.

"We made love and promises all morning. We were going to unite our lives back at the Halls. We really *did* love each other."

"But…?"

"But we missed the Fend Cup."

"That's unfortunate."

"More than you think. You see, we didn't know this was going to happen, but by not being there to record the story, it never happened. We had irrevocably changed time. That was when Miranda realized it."

"What did she realize?"

"Well, she had an immediate sense that something was wrong. She's keen like that. It terrified her when she began thinking about what the consequences were to be. Without us there, the memory couldn't happen, and world peace was never achieved. It was one of the simple principles of consciousness, and one we should not have forgotten."

"So, what happened then?"

"We returned back to the Halls to take our licks."

"What do they do for stuff like that?"

"You might be executed." Vaks picked up the spilled glass and poured more whiskey into it. "They put me in the Chamber of Reflection for three days. That was the extent of the punishment though. I think that they showed mercy because it was my first time, but it was such a serious offense that I was never the same after it. Mostly due to the time in the Chamber of Reflection though."

That was when Entropy started talking back to me.

"What was it like?"

"The Chamber of Reflection?"

Javier nodded.

"Pure darkness. Pure silence."

Javier was quiet.

"I came out of that place a very different person."

"I can imagine." They paused as Javier refilled his whiskey. "What about Miranda? Did you ever see her again?"

"Sure, I saw her again, but we never spoke much anymore. I never learned what her punishment was, but she took pains to avoid me, and I let her."

"What about those promises you had made to her?"

"They remain the petroglyphs of past lives."

"Hmmm," Javier said, stroking his mustache. "I don't know how you can make even a happy Story like that bitter and dry. After all, you were at the Fend Cup!"

"Maybe it's because I just held the corpse of my eviscerated son a few weeks ago."

Javier nearly spit out his whiskey.

"Oh, my God!" He exclaimed, coughing violently and hammering his fist into his chest.

Vaks did not change his expression.

"What happened?" Javier gasped out hoarsely through his coughing.

"I left Jal and went back to the Halls of Remembrance."

"Wait, wait, wait, you went back just like that?"

"It didn't take me long to realize that whatever love I had on Jal before, was dead now." Vaks sighed. "Just like that, I went back to the Halls of Remembrance."

Chapter 12 - Murder

Gasping from the reflex response of traveling, Vaks manifested onto the stone courtyard outside of the Halls of Remembrance. His face was a contortion of rage and hurt. His vision was blurry and wet. He noticed first that there was something strange about the sand beneath his feet. It was moist.

Looking down, his vision took on a pink tinge. As it cleared, Vaks saw that the yellow sand had congealed with running blood.

His stomach experienced a vacuum.

The blood traced to a corpse several paces away.

Vaks ran over, but it was clear the man was well dead. His throat had been cut half through, and the spinal cord was exposed. Looking up, Vaks saw another body sprawled over the stone steps, the head hanging grotesquely open with the gaping wound. A mask of blood covered the face of the man as it ran down the steps and collected in the sands.

The banners whipped in the wind, cracking the silence of death. He approached the Great Hall, the butchered bodies around him. It seemed a nightmare had forced its way into reality. The people appeared as if they were killed exactly where they stood, none of them falling back for reinforcements or showing signs of resistance.

The weapon the killer had used caused so much carnage that Vaks' feet stuck to the mosaic temple courtyard as he made his way inside. He called out, but Vaks heard only the moan of wind and the patter of dropping blood in reply. Vaks knew what he would find before he walked into the nursery. Every child in every crib, bed, or chair was murdered just the same.

Vaks vomited.

Grasping for something real and tangible, he refused to believe this reality. Tears streamed down his face, and he found the stone walls and let them brace him as he wept. This couldn't be real. He didn't have to believe it. This was just the hallucinations getting out of control. This is just what happens when Entropy goes on untreated by the StoryTellers; they start hallucinating and losing their minds.

They aren't really dead, Vaks told himself, but the smell of death in the air proved otherwise. He wept, his eyes closed, emotions of rage and loss washing over him. He was terrified and furious, and needed to know what had happened.

He was going to find out who was responsible for this and pull their intestines through their throat. Something warmed in him as he thought this. A burst of strength ran through his body. Vaks turned around and followed the trail of corpses. The killer had left his footprints in the blood.

He was making his way toward the Pools of Memory, methodically going through each room, checking for survivors. There were none. Some deeper inside the temple had taken weapons from the armory he saw, but to no avail. They littered the Temple with their eviscerated remains.

Vaks hunted the path like a savage wolf, the darkness closing in around the edges of his vision. The shock of the situation threatened his sanity with increasing alarm, Entropy's voice egging him on.

That's right, Vaks, find the murderer...find him and kill him... Look at how many lives he took! Look at how needlessly they died! Surrender Vaks...surrender to my name, and I will give you the power to kill the one responsible.

Vaks salivated at the sound of the words. They were ripe and full of promise. He could bite into one and its juice would spray out. The voice of Entropy was promising something that Vaks could not properly describe. It was the culmination of his desires contained in a wave of energy that he felt only when talking to Entropy.

Become my servant, Vaks, and take me to the Edge of Time. There, your murderer waits.

He reached the end of the footprints at the Vials of Sand. Whoever was responsible for this was a StoryTeller. They had to be if they were using the Sands of Time. But where would they go to?

Stepping out from the shadows was the lurching form of Entropy. It strolled across the room and put a comforting hand on Vaks' face. He could not contain himself and fell to weeping into its open palm.

"There, there," the demon said. "It's not so bad. At least now you can start life over again. Not everyone gets that chance, you know?"

Vaks said nothing. What good would it do to talk to something that wasn't actually there?

"Come on, Vaks, I know where the killer is. He's waiting for you. He knows one more is going to chase him, and he plans to kill you."

"Why does he want to kill the StoryTellers?" Vaks asked, his eyes red with tears.

"You'll have to ask him yourself."

There were over a hundred dead men, women, and children at the Halls of Remembrance, and only because Vaks had gone to Jal so quickly had he missed the massacre.

"Why the Edge of Time?" Vaks asked Entropy, slowly letting go of his sanity. He was about to give in to the urges of his hallucinations and cross a line from which he could never return. By swallowing the Sand required to travel to the Edge of Time, he would have none to come home with. The nature of the Sands worked through a series of calculations that related the time and location of their effect, to the percent that a person was carrying after, and what was consumed before. By consuming 100 percent of one's Sand, there would not be a single grain by which to return to the Halls of Remembrance with.

It was a theoretical end which had been tested by StoryTellers in the past who had never returned.

Do it, Vaks. Leave the universe behind.

What if someone had survived? The thought struck him like a lightning bolt. He couldn't know for sure unless he counted.

Your killer won't wait for long, Vaks…

Vaks set down the vial of Sand and took a sheet of parchment from a desk drawer. He dipped his finger in the blood pooling at his feet and traced the words "Edge of Time" onto the paper.

Wiping the blood off on his pant leg, Vaks tightened his satchel about his torso, still packed for Traveling from Jal. If there was anyone left alive they would find the note and follow him to the Edge of Time. If there was no one left alive, then it wouldn't matter at all what he did. It didn't matter either way. There was nothing at all that would matter to him ever again.

Seething with rage, despair, and the eclipsing obliteration of existence as he knew it, Vaks opened the vial of Sand and consumed every grain.

Chapter 13 - Shammal the Killer

Shammal had been waiting for several hours in the desert. It wasn't a long time by any real stretch, but it was long enough to tire him of waiting. Despite his anxiousness to meet the survivor, Shammal was enjoying a profound sense of peace that he had not felt in a great many years.

He recalled a time during his youth when he would walk with his mother down to the well. It was a time when there was a magic and limitlessness to life that made him giggle with excitement. He'd catch frogs there and release them into the river on their way back home.

Shammal's favorite part of those days was the smell of baking cookies his mother would often make. He could have one cookie if he ate his vegetables, two if he did something especially good that day, and none if he was naughty. He always tried very hard to be good. When he had a naughty day, it tore him apart because he missed out on those cookies. He'd give anything to keep a naughty day from happening.

Shammal hadn't seen his mother in over eighteen years. He left her when he was thirteen after she had tried to sell him to a pimp to pay for her addictions. Shammal managed to pinch the knife off the belt of one of his captors as he was pretending to be docile and compliant, stabbed him in the leg, and bolted out of a window. They never caught him.

It was strange to be thinking of his mother now. Shammal hadn't often thought of her at all, except when he was particularly angry and wanted to throw out some deliciously explicit language. It fit after all, considering his judgement was coming. His deliverer would soon render his spirit free from the flesh. He had waited a long time for this.

Shammal never did have a choice. Not after he crossed the murder line the first time. He never understood what the big deal was about it. Another murder, another fewer life in the world, another less mouth consuming resources. Besides, they were all toast anyway. There was no sense in taking crap from people just because they didn't want to share their food supply.

They apprehended him after he and a gang of his killed an entire hospital to get their hands on the drugs. He was put in subthermal isolation, which would keep him frozen and asleep until the end of the planet came.

No one was expecting the A.I. to turn though, and when they did, they corrupted a lot of the technology on the planet. One of the systems they sabotaged was the sub-thermal prison. Their corrupting virus spread into the reanimation protocols that brought Shammal back to life, twisting his mind more grotesquely.

During his life, Shammal committed terrible acts to both survive, and serve the strange motivations that drove him. He took no companions, except for a woman when he wanted, and even then, they always returned from his bed shaken and traumatized. Shammal did not think like normal people thought. His brain had been tampered with during his sleep, and when he started talking to himself, he was actually hearing the voices of the universe speaking back to him.

This drove him mad over the years as he fled capture by his victims' families, and eventually he found himself protected in the religious movement of the Enlightened Story. He could renounce his sins and live a new life, take a new name, and after some time, would be forgotten by the rest of the world.

This was, in fact, the case, but his evil hallucinations seemed not to be confined to his own mind. During his meditations, he felt the dark thoughts evict themselves from his mind and go into the cells of fellow acolytes, corrupting them. His presence was the poison of Entropy, and the Enlightened Story soon began sowing dissent and rumors of corruption throughout the land.

A division occurred in the people between the supporters of the religion and otherwise, and soon there was a distinct separation between the two states, with plenty of bad blood between them.

Shammal's meditations were profound experiences of darkness. He could do nothing to change the fact that every time he entered into a trance, he was consumed by a need to tear apart the bonding elements of the universe, destroying structure where it stands.

Shammal sighed. His bones were weary, his mind heavy. He was getting old and life was weighing on him more than he could bear. Voices were screaming in his ears.

Get up, you filthy wretch! You weak human meat pile, get your pitiful excuse for existence up and do your work! You are too weak to be my savior. The real champion will end your misery. He's coming now to slit your gut, you failure.

The words were nails into his flesh, but Shammal was undisturbed. Words were nothing to him now. He had seen the peaks of heaven and the hot fires of hell. He had been a savior and the harbinger of death. He was not one to be taken so easily by the words of his demon mind.

They had led him to the Halls of Remembrance though. They had led him to Alastair Godric, the StoryTeller, the man who had founded the Enlightened Story. He was the real reason why Shammal was there. Not because Alastair or any one of them in that foolish group that sent him were worth a damn, but because he knew that they were right about the Story. It was the StoryTellers who had botched the whole universe to begin with.

That was what was so wrong about the whole thing. The reason everyone was clinging to life on this unstable rock was because the StoryTellers had tipped the universe off balance and initiated the Entropy Cycle.

Shammal knew that if he could go back, he could stop them. It might make a difference. It might put an end to everything before the end begins. Then he wouldn't have to exist, and the universe wouldn't ever have to justify bringing something as evil and wretched as he into being. After all, if it weren't for him, his mother would still be alive.

He appeared out of the night, just as Shammal had expected him too. He was also as enraged as Shammal had expected him to be. The dark-haired man, hands clenched in bloody fists, pierced Shammal with such a furious glare that he almost wet his pants with excitement.

He didn't care; this was the end of his life. This was when he could die. The voices promised him he could die here. They promised him if he killed the StoryTellers, a survivor would follow him through and kill him in return.

Shammal didn't have a chance to speak. The survivor struck him in the chin with his knee and was soon pinning him to the dirt, slicing the flesh across his brow, and tearing the scalp from Shammal's body. The man screamed savagely, his pupils dilating the entire surface of his eyes. His hands were frightfully strong, superhuman in their fury.

"Wait..." Shammal uttered through a gasping breath that spouted out a broken tooth.

The man stopped, the blade hovering over Shammal's heart. Blood dripped from his fist, the bloody scalp in the same hand as the knife.

"Kill me, yes...but first..." He coughed blood and mucus out of his mouth. "Know this: Alastair sent me. Seek the StoryTeller who wants you dead; your vengeance is with him."

The words must have had an impression on the man because he fell backwards, scrambling up to his feet, releasing Shammal.

"What?"

Shammal slowly got to his feet, a long tendril of blood stretching from his mouth to the desert sand. "Alastair. He was a StoryTeller of the third generation."

That had quite the effect on the survivor. Shammal was surprised by this. He didn't understand everything that Alastair had taught about the StoryTellers, but saying his title like that had a strange effect on the man who was supposed to deliver him from life.

"Why did you do it?" He could barely whisper the words through his emotions.

"Because your kind is a scourge. You must be exterminated before you destroy everything." Shammal spat, sending flashes of pain through his vision. "I'd kill you too if I had anything left in me."

The man leapt forward and thrust the knife into Shammal's chest, his fist colliding with such force that Shammal expelled his bodily fluids and went crashing to the ground.

The man held his attention on Shammal's dying eyes and gazed inward with abominable darkness.

Shammal spat on his killer. It was the last thing that he experienced because the blade that had sliced through his flesh had penetrated his heart, denying him further life. Shammal Dadra, bane of StoryTellers, was dead.

PART II
THE EDGE OF TIME

Chapter 14 - Suspicions

"Here," Javier said, offering to refill Vaks' whiskey.

"No!" Vaks said, woozily waving a hand over his glass. "S'already full!"

Javier grumbled and then stood up, shaking nervously on his legs as he stabilized himself with the edge of the table.

Vaks had consumed a copious amount of alcohol over the course of the conversation. He was not one to turn down a drink, and had a reputation for being one of the serious drinkers at the Halls of Remembrance. He could outdrink just about anyone there—except for the super alcoholics, that is. They committed their bodies to alcohol much more than Vaks was willing, often dying young from the abuse. Despite their differences, Vaks was well received among the alcoholics nonetheless.

Aware of his relationship to the poison that brought him as much pleasure as it did, Vaks drank heavily, but not in such a manner that it destroyed what he loved. Consequently, when Javier had offered him another shot of whiskey, Vaks became unsure of how much more he really wanted to handle.

The man had been going drink for drink with him all night, and any ordinary fellow would be on the floor by now. Vaks didn't realize he was going to be sitting down with an expert drinker this morning when he woke up—let alone be alive.

The sun had set some time ago, and the chill of oblivion set upon the land in all its starless terror. This night had become familiar to Vaks. It haunted him in the utter totality of its darkness. This really was the end.

They had nearly finished two bottles of whiskey, and still Javier did not show any signs of slowing down. It seemed he meant to drink himself into a stupor, which was a point Vaks did not want to reach.

"So, we go to Cantor and ask around! Someone has to know where Alastair is!" Javier exclaimed, taking a drink straight from the bottle and slamming it down on the table.

Vaks looked up at him, but said nothing.

"I mean you want to find this—*hic*—guy, don't you?" Javier walked over to the door and kicked it open. The warm glow from inside spilled out into an arc of light across the desert sand.

Vaks nodded to him.

"Then we need to go to Cantor and find out what they know about Alastair." He pointed a finger toward the darkness. "There has got to be someone there who'll tell us where to find him. That's the *city* man; there isn't another place like it in the entire universe. I haven't been in a year though…"

"Hold on a second," Vaks said, standing up. "You shouldn't come with me. I've got a dark shadow haunting my way, Javier. You want no part in it."

"Hogwash!" Javier snorted, walking back toward the table, his shoulders hunched with exhaustion. He reached for the bottle and took another drink. "You need me out here! No one knows this place better than—*hic*—I…" He looked like he had just triumphantly swallowed a rebellious creature back into his stomach. "Sure, I maybe haven't been out of the house for some time, but it doesn't mean that I forgot all I know about this world!"

"Thank you, Javier; but really, I must do this alone."

"Pfffft! You kids and your selfishness. One of these days you are going to realize something about life." He leaned in toward Vaks, his eye widening and his lip raising to reveal a pointed canine. "We're all connected together, all the meat and all the mind."

Vaks crossed his arms and scrutinized Javier.

"Look," Javier said, pulling back and taking on a less imposing appearance. "This world is damn near at the end of its rope. Strange things have been happening. I don't know what's going to happen to us. Maybe we should have died with the rest of the universe. I don't know. But what I do know…what I do know is that what's happened to you is significant, Vaks. I don't need to be a Necrodian to know that. You are part of something very important, and I want to help see it through."

Vaks eyed Javier for a moment, and then, releasing the tension he was holding with his body, sighed.

"Look, I can help you," Javier said earnestly. "I know about this world. You clearly have no idea what's in store for you. You haven't seen what the rest of this place is like. You are going to need some help with that."

"Why?"

Javier's face dropped with his shoulders. He suddenly looked weary and old. "Because I've lived a long time, Vaks. The only reason I've lived so long a time is because I've avoided involving myself directly in a lot of what's happened. I don't want to do that anymore. I can help you, and I don't care about the dangers, but I need to do something good with my life. One thing, anything, as long as it's good."

"Okay."

Javier brightened, lifting the bottle in the air with celebration. "To you, Vaks, and the journey ahead of us." He paused to take another drink and Vaks could hardly believe that the man was still standing. "We may be at the Edge of Time Vaks, but the end is…"

Javier stopped midsentence and collapsed onto the wooden floorboards in a snoring heap. Standing in his place was the shadowy form of Entropy, grinning and rubbing its hands. It backed away and melted into the shadows, fusing itself into a two-dimensional apparition, walking along the surface of the wall, making faces at Vaks.

Its black teeth protruded from alabaster gums like a Venus flytrap. Its face was so pliant and expressive, it seemed that it could contort its features into any grotesque array. Vaks ignored it at the moment, woozily walking over to Javier and grabbing hold of his boots. He straightened Javier's body out so that he wasn't crumpled up on himself, and went to get a blanket from the bedroom.

Vaks tossed the blanket over the snoring body of Javier, put the whiskey bottle on the counter, which had mostly spilled during the fall, and returned to his cot. Each step was harder than the last, the weight of the Story overwhelming his mind. Entropy's elongated fingers pulled back the blanket on the cot as Vaks laid down.

"Alastair…" he muttered drunkenly. "You took everything from me." He adjusted himself to a more comfortable position. "I'm going to bash your skull in."

Entropy's fingers stroked Vaks' hair, the glossy black nails sliding across his scalp. A smile crept across his face as Vaks plunged into sleep.

Vaks woke to the roaring thunder of machines pounding outside. He bolted upright from the cot and sprang to his feet. The world followed him as he became immediately aware of his lingering drunkenness. Shaking his head, Vaks tried to clear his vision, but all he could see were vague, blurry shapes outside the windows of Javier's home.

Javier was still asleep on the wooden floor. He didn't look like he had moved at all. He looked frighteningly still for a moment, but Vaks saw a twitch in his chest as he made his way across the room.

"*Javier!*" Vaks whispered, kicking him in the boots.

Javier didn't move. Vaks took another look out the window and could see clearer now. There were three short, lanky creatures dismounting cyborg horses and unsheathing weapons.

"*Javier!!!*" Vaks whispered again, kicking much harder into his thigh. Javier yelped and scrambled to his feet, spewing obscenities. His face was red and swollen, and he whirled around looking for his attacker.

His antics had gotten the attention of the horrific creatures strapped in leather, one shrieking as it bolted toward the door, brandishing some jagged implement.

Vaks smacked Javier firmly across the head and pointed out the front window.

Seeing the imminent danger, Javier and Vaks leapt onto their stomachs behind a row of shelves.

"*What the heck is that thing!*" Vaks whispered.

The door crashed inwards, and the war cry that followed was as the very power that splintered those hinges.

Vaks clenched in alarm, biting his cheek and spilling blood.

Javier was stretching his eyes open, yawning his jaw, and shaking off whatever alcohol he could in the precious few moments they had before they were discovered.

"Mutants."

"What's the plan?" Vaks asked, already certain what the answer was.

The mutant had halted in the center of the dining room and was sniffing loudly about.

"We're going to have to kill them." There was a small crash of glassware shattering.

"Do you have any weapons?"

"Here, take this…"

A boot slammed against a table and sent it scraping across the floor and into the wall. A rapid clicking sound filled the air.

Vaks paled. "What the hell is a mutant?"

"Exactly what you think it is."

Vaks swallowed as he took the hammer that Javier passed to him. He looked at it with grim resolve. His knife was over in his satchel across the room if he needed it. A growl issued forth that vibrated the floorboards.

A hand scraped across the wood, and Vaks could hear ragged breathing. Adrenaline went rushing through him. He could hear the weight of the mutant on the countertop, leaning across it, sniffing the air with long, moist inhales.

Javier was gripping a small iron club that had been modified with welded black crystals to improve its use as a beating implement.

Just as the mutant had no idea of what was waiting for him when its bulging forehead passed through the plane of view, Vaks knew by the vacuum of the moment that battle had begun.

Javier's club came swinging up in an obliterating arc that collided with the head of the mutant. Crystal pressed itself onto flesh, breaking bone, and destroying brain tissue as blood splattered out.

The mutant released a horrific scream, that was immediately silenced by death, which followed abruptly after its sounding. The silence was answered by the infuriated roars of the others.

"GO!" Javier shouted, shoving Vaks in the opposite direction he was headed.

A claw scraped across the wooden countertop, and a soaring body launched through the air, bounding off the wall as it twisted itself around, screeching through its hideous maw.

It stood on two lean human legs strapped in black leather, though not resembling much humanity at the feet. Extra toes sprouted off their bare soles like warts, each with a pointed claw. Its shins were too long, wound with tuber-like tendons stretching into muscles. The head was grotesque, sending Vaks scrambling back in fear. He lost his footing and fell backward.

Putrid steam escaped the mutant's drooling bat maw as Vaks was rolling forward toward the balls of his feet. It roared in defiance. Vaks could see in the mutant's mouth. The teeth were needles arranged in rows extending down the throat.

Tendons tensed, coiling into themselves. The mutant sprang toward Vaks with two clawed hands grasping outward. Vaks uncoiled toward the mutant, swinging his arm in a forward arc, the hammer at the fulcrum. It had no eyes, but instead had a bulging mass of flesh that protruded out of its forehead and down to its animal nose.

The hammer collided with the bulging mass and produced a wet thud, stopping the mutant's momentum with a small burst of blood.

Its carcass crashed onto Vaks' thighs, a claw spasming outward and lacerating his leg. Vaks kicked it squarely aside and gripped his leg.

Javier cried out in pain. A shrieking hiss filled through the room. Vaks was on his feet focusing on the mutant pinning Javier to the ground. He threw the hammer and watched it collide with the top of the mutant's head as it reared back, shrieking with a flexed claw. Javier seized the opportunity of the creatures disorientation to grip it by the throat and leverage his force through his weapon.

"ARRRGGGHHH!!!!" Javier screamed, as his club swung upward. Red and blue liquid arced off the crystals with each thump. Silence slowly refilled the air as the beating stopped and the creature fell dead to the side.

The club dropped to the wooden floorboards, and now, only over the heavy panting of Javier, and the occasional click from the dying mutant, could Vaks focus on his own beating heart.

Chapter 15 - Resistance

Cartin Delgado took well to the streets of Cantor, but it had not been easy for her at first. She suffered severe depression and pondered often whether or not she'd be better off dead. Her prospects at life were bleak it seemed, and most people only offered to help her in exchange for sex. It made her want to commit suicide, and she often considered visiting the Death Specialists to help her facilitate it.

She was living in a single cubicle, using the money her rescuers gave her to pay for the rent. It had a single window, high in the corner, with no opening by which to let air in or out. It was not a safe place to live, but for the price of it, she would be able to stay for a couple months until she found work. That was what she found most difficult about life in Cantor. Most everyone she inquired about work with sent her straight to the brothels to be a prostitute. Cartin decided at once that she would not resort to that for survival, even if she starved to death.

Other places weren't interested in her simply because she had no references or skills that she could market. She could mine ore better than just about anybody in Cantor, but nobody needed that right now. It didn't help that every day when Cartin woke up she thought about ways to destroy the Governor of Cantor and all of his corrupt network. She was growing more bitter and venomous each day.

She tried to tell people that her entire colony was murdered by the Governor's orders, but no one cared more than to buy her a drink. Everyone already seemed to know that the Governor was a crook, and most had heard stories much worse than what had happened to Cartin.

It was a dry afternoon, and Cartin was lounging on the porch of the tavern sipping whiskey and watching the passersby. There were mutants, less twisted than those creatures running feral in the wild, but still dangerous. There were sentient species that had migrated to the Edge of Time from other galaxies before the Ragnarok Wave, but it seemed that they were always traveling through. They passed the inner gates toward the city sector of Cantor where the wealthy and prosperous citizens of the Edge of Time dwelt.

She enjoyed watching life walk by in front of the tavern. You never knew who you were going to see, and what they were going to be up to. Cartin was eyeing a dusty traveler towing a cart full of scavenge he had collected and considered taking on the profession of scavenging herself. It'd be difficult without a vehicle, and she didn't know of any crews that were hiring, let alone where to contact one. She took a drink of her whiskey as the cart passed by, followed by a traveler bearing the Emblem of the Story around his neck. She had been seeing more and more of those lately.

It was a normal day in front of the tavern, but in the alleyway beside it, there came a high scream. She whipped her head in the direction and stood up from her seat, walking over to the railing so she could peer around the other side. There was a thud, followed by a breathless grunt. There, a young man was getting beat to death by three of the Governors' enforcers.

Cartin leapt the railing deftly and rushed to his aid, blindsiding one of the enforcers with a powerful shoulder charge that sent him careening over. The other whipped around to face her, seething with rage. The victim's blood was speckled on his face.

"Got a problem with a fair fight?" Cartin hissed.

The lead man grinned as the other scrambled back to his feet muttering curses, his face reddening.

"Got a problem minding your own business?" he said.

"Yeah," Cartin barked. "Not only that, but I got a problem minding bullies too!" She crossed her arms over her chest. She didn't like the way he was leering at her.

"Come on, miss, no need to go giving me a reason to arrest you." The enforcer licked his lips and grinned. "We could just get together on our own." He gave the hurt man a firm kick and took a step toward Cartin.

Cartin sprung forward faster than his mind could parse; her metal knuckles crushed into his helmet, shattering through the cyber-glass visor. Shards flew outward, cutting her cheek. Her metal knuckles did not stop at the flesh, punishing through to the bone. Blood, teeth, and brain ejected out of the enforcer's head as her fist passed through it.

Cartin's eyes widened with surprise as her arm came to a stop. The man on the ground screamed as shards of cyberglass impaled into him, shattered from the impact of her fist.

Blood and brain matter dripped off the spherical joints connecting the cylinders that replaced her tendons. She looked up, unaware until this very moment how dangerous the ramifications of having a cybernetic arm attached could be.

The other two enforcers backed away, their feet scraping the tensing silence.

Cartin Delgado narrowed her eyes.

"Get lost," she snarled.

They turned and ran out down the far end of the alley away

from Cartin.

She turned her gaze to the fallen man and knelt beside him, gently examining his wounds.

The man winced as he was straining to position himself upright. He grunted with pain and clutched his torso where a shard of cyberglass had stuck.

Cartin eased his hand and pulled the shard out from him, pressing his hand on the wound. "Can you walk?"

He nodded and started lifting his body upward. Cartin helped him, and he was soon on his feet. His face was bleeding, and his ribs were hurt from more than the shard of glass, but he appeared mobile enough to keep a steady pace. "Come on," he said, "I know of a safe place to get to before they come back. We don't have much time." He looked at Cartin with a cunning grin. "You don't know it yet, but right now, you are just as lucky as I am that you saved me."

"What do you mean?"

"Come on. We'd better just get someplace safe right now before anything else."

The man turned and started walking out of the alley. Soon he was on the main street and Cartin had to run several paces to catch up with him. "Wait! What's your name?"

"It doesn't matter what my name is right now; just stay focused on what's around you and follow." There was a degree of severity in his voice that reminded Cartin of what the mine boss sounded like when he reprimanded reckless miners who disregarded safety.

Cartin held her tongue and followed. They weaved through the crowds that milled about. Distant cries of fights echoed through the chatter and bustle of the cesspool of life that was Cantor's outskirts.

Steam spiraled upward like dust devils above the hovels. There it cast itself outwards into morphing clouds that constituted the hazy sky. They passed merchants selling cuts of meat, the aroma ominous, the nature of the meat suspect. He turned sharply through a jet of steam, Cartin followed, the warm air invigorating her.

They were in an alley and the man banged his fist on a metal door so rusted and corroded by the damp air that clouds of oxidized sediment floated off it. The banging reverberated inside. A metal latch slid open, and Cartin couldn't see the eyes that were peering through. The latch shut closed, and a lock turned.

The door groaned open, and a chitinous creature stood before them. Four-armed and massive, its entire body was covered in a thick-plated chitinous exoskeleton. Cartin had not seen an actinid in real life, but she knew how to recognize one immediately. How could she not remember the stories of the savage actinid warriors who slew by the hundreds?

The natural actinid lived in quadrant seven, but once the earthquakes shook loose the foundations of their atmospheric protection, their vapors equalized with the air of human habitation with apocalyptic results. The reaction was pure annihilation. At a rate faster than an actinid could fly, the air became utterly hostile to them, eradicating their species and petrifying their flesh in an instant.

The only survivors were the descended few of those actinids who chose to splice their genetic composition with that of humans and become a hybrid species which could live in a human habitat. The earthquake was a result of the AI revolt, and along with the actinid destruction, most of the human population was killed. The fractured remains of intergalactic life that were the survivors collected in Cantor and prepared for the end.

It was technology of that caliber that created the Edge of Time to begin with. Technology that was stored in the webwork of the Netmind, forever lost after the revolt.

Here Cartin was seeing an actinid in real life. Living proof of genetic re-creation. They were even more terrifying to behold than she imagined.

"What delayed you?" Its voice was a rapid series of clicks and tones, like a ringing telephone crossed with a cricket.

"Enforcers caught me. Beat me near dead. She found me, took care of the enforcers...now let's move." The man's voice was ragged and pained.

The actinid took a surveying glance of the wounded man and the gore drenched arm of Cartin and moved aside. "All the crew is ready for evacuation," he said. Cartin wasn't sure whether it was a male or female of its kind, but by the look of the mandibles, she didn't want to find out either.

"I should have told you this beforehand..." the man said, turning to look at Cartin before opening a second door inside the shabby building. "You aren't going to be allowed to leave here. You've already seen too much. I hope it doesn't pose too much of a problem."

Cartin gritted her teeth, the metal between the joints of her fist tightening. If she wanted to leave, she was going to do it. Nevertheless, she hadn't seen any reason other than his apparent means of kidnapping her to seem dangerous, so she was willing to follow him another step at the very least, even if she knew there was not going to be a step back.

The door opened into a room just as shabby as the last, except for the fact that stacked against the walls were rows of humming computer equipment and machines. Wires ran like wild roots across the floor, pumping electricity through their veins.

"Sir!" A woman gasped, seeing the beaten man open the door. "Benson, get the first aid kit now!"

"Helga, it's alright, I assure you," he said.

"Shut your mouth and sit down." Helga pulled a chair from the corner and set it next to the lamp in the corner of the room. "Come on now. I have to fix you up before we jump."

Grumbling, the man walked over and sat down in the chair. Cartin followed him and stood close by.

"My name is Wilcox by the way," he said. "Captain Wilcox."

"Captain? Of what?"

"Of the Life of Time Resistance."

"The what?" Cartin asked, fighting the urge to touch the sticky blood on her arm.

"Helga, get someone to clean up...I'm sorry what's your name?"

"Cartin Delgado."

"Someone to clean up Miss Delgado." Helga snapped her fingers, and one of the soldiers stepped out of the room to carry out the order. "Pleased to meet you, Miss Delgado. We have a few minutes, but just a few. Helga here can patch me up faster than anyone else alive, and we need all the time we can spare. Enforcers will be here any minute."

"You think they are on to us already?"

Wilcox laughed. "Are you kidding me? Have you really never heard of LTR before?"

Cartin shook her head.

He scoffed. "Well we are fighting against it. All of it. Every last bit of ground that scum-sucking, slippery, cod-skin, manure heap of a Governor stands on is going to drink his blood."

"And the blood of his followers," Helga chimed in.

Cartin held her tongue, though she felt the fire of her own rage and determination blaze inside her. So the worm had other enemies too.

"As it is, we are a major threat to them now that their Blue Blood factories are caput."

A jolt of panic seized Cartin. She was going to need Blue Blood! Once the morphing process was complete, and the cybernetic arm was fused fully with every other part of her body, she would be dependent on synthetic Blue Blood to survive any blood loss she experienced.

"Don't worry," Wilcox said, "the reason we destroyed the factories is because the Governor was putting a certain sedative into the blood supply in order to calm down his patrons. He was addicting them and keeping himself in power and drugging every cyborg with his watered-down poisoned goo."

"You mean to tell me that he's been poisoning the Cyborg population's life source?"

Wilcox nodded. "We are going to make more of it though, because when we broke into the laboratory, I lifted the ingredients for the concoction. It seems simple enough without the poisons. It's starting a war, really. He's not going to let us become the city's biggest supplier of Blood, but we're going to do it anyway."

Chapter 16 - The Elder 'Borgs

Vaks hastened over to Javier. He was groaning in the pooling blood of a mutant corpse. His hands clutched his stomach, which had been severely lacerated by a rusty meat hook.

Fountains of blue liquid spurted between Javier's trembling fingers.

"Dammit!" Javier growled. "The bugger got me good. This is gonna take the last of my stores."

"Tell me what you need."

Javier mumbled a curse and said, "in the bedroom, underneath the bed, there's a metal case. I need you to bring that to me." He coughed blue liquid onto his lips. His skin was paling.

Vaks nodded and went through the bedroom door without hesitation. He knelt down to retrieve the briefcase and saw gleaming yellow eyes.

They widened, the slits of black focusing in on Vaks' terror. Entropy's Venus flytrap maw of jagged needle teeth sprang open and outward.

Vaks screamed, falling backward onto the wooden floor, heart beating.

"What's going on in there!" Javier's labored cry beckoned.

"Nothing, just slipped!" Vaks called back, rolling over to his feet, growling curses at Entropy.

"Slipped!?" came Javier's exasperated voice.

Entropy sat on the floor, his spiny back resting against the bed frame. It was picking its teeth with an elongated finger sharpened into a fine tip.

Vaks growled at the shadowy thing and grabbed the case underneath the bed. He stood up, paying Entropy no mind.

"Well done, killing those mutants," Entropy said.

Vaks stopped and turned around, making eye contact with the demon who was now standing his full stature. Entropy grinned again, the awful display of teeth and terror making a ghastly visage surfeit with arrogance and mockery toward Vaks.

Javier groaned from the other room, and Vaks hastened out, leaving Entropy and its bitterness behind him.

"What the hell took you so long?" Javier groused as Vaks attempted to open the latches on the case. They wouldn't budge.

"Leave it," Javier said, "It needs my touch." He reached for the latch and opened it. The case revealed a multi-tiered structure filled with various mechanical parts. Javier grabbed a suture torch from inside the case and began searing his stomach shut, screaming as he did so. His hand trembled and gave out. He looked pleadingly at Vaks.

When Vaks had completed suturing with the torch, Javier took a package of blue liquid from a row of sleeves, which were all now vacant. A needle tip on one end of the package enabled Javier to slam it into his thigh and drain the contents into his blood stream.

"Blue Blood," he sighed, his head leaning back in bliss. "This stuff is liquid life I tell you what." The bag was empty, and Javier threw it across the room. He took another breath and closed his eyes for a long contemplative moment. When he opened them he saw

Vaks looking intently for what he was going to say.

"That was my last pouch," Javier said despairingly.

"Can you get more?"

He shook his head. "Not unless I get to Cantor. They synthesize a compound there that is acceptable, but it is nothing like the pure stuff. That was the last of it. Probably the last one of stuff *that pure* that I'll find anywhere."

"Right…so, are you going to be okay?"

Javier gave Vaks a cold look. "My guts just got sliced open, seared shut, and now I have to answer the question if I'm okay?"

"Well, if you don't want to answer…"

"Naw, I'm fine. I just thought I'd mess with you. You aren't as fun as the other ones."

"What are you talking about? What other ones?"

"Never mind that; I expect you want to know about the Blue Blood now, yeah?"

Vaks nodded slowly, his jaw tense.

"It is the very life blood of a cyborg. When a DNA pairing with a cybernetic system occurs and is successful, the body eventually replaces all human blood with cyborg blood. This only happens once, and once the body has fully integrated a full body's blood supply, it will not induce the creation of human blood ever again. If you lose some, you have to refill it from an outside source."

"Jesus…"

Javier raised an eyebrow. "I didn't take you for a man of religion."

"I'm not, but…I guess it's just a bad habit. I've never seen a cyborg like you before. I mean, I would have never even guessed that you weren't human at all."

"I *am* human."

"Right, but you know what I mean."

"Yeah, but you have no idea what *I* mean."

Javier was getting to his feet, completely unfazed by the laceration through his gut. He walked over to the liquor cabinet and swung open the door. He grabbed a bottle of whiskey and bit the cork out, spitting it back onto the dusty shelves. He drank straight from the bottle, gulping three long swallows.

"God, I tell you, the most remarkable thing about being a Genesis cyborg is the fact that I can still get drunk." He offered the bottle to Vaks, who took it, taking a moderate swig of poison.

"What exactly is a Genesis cyborg?"

Javier looked at Vaks with astonishment. "You guys are supposed to have the entire cosmos's history contained in the memories of your Halls, and you're telling me you haven't heard about the Genesis cyborgs?"

"Do you have any idea how much information that actually is?" Vaks retorted. "We learn fundamentals and what we must in the capacity of our nature, but all of it? That's for the Elders. They're supposed to have a trick for that."

Javier rolled his eyes and let it pass. "It was a big event though, the cyborg Genesis. It changed the course of the universe and was the only reason why we were able to construct the Edge of Time to begin with."

"Wait a minute..."

"What?"

"You helped construct the Edge of Time?"

Javier sighed and took a seat at the same table they had drank at the night before and gestured for Vaks to join him. Vaks looked at the corpses littering the floor, the oozing liquids, and the encroaching stench.

"Don't worry, this won't take long. I'll take you to Cantor after. I have business there to get some Blue Blood now. I just want you to understand something about this place. I am not going to take it lightly that a StoryTeller should wind up at *my* estate of all places. It can't be coincidence."

"Coincidence?"

Javier nodded. "I'm an Elder 'Borg, Vaks. I've lived a *long* time. More than you think even now. Thousands of years, but beyond that, I am the prototype by which all 'Borgs were made."

Chapter 17 - Prototype

Javier was a young man once. His surname was, and still is, Estolla. He was thirty-three years old, the proud owner of a grungy bar in the humid Harriet Understreets, and a bachelor with no regrets. The Harriet Understreets were underneath the Skycaps, whose urban spires housed the executive and science classes of the planet.

Javier was neither an executive nor a scientist, nor did he have any desire to be either of them. He was a bar owner who had dropped out of engineering school when he realized he could live a comfortable life serving drinks to the neighbors in his cubic block.

Javier was one of three trillion citizens of the most advanced civilization in the art of crafting artificial intelligence systems. His was a planet that exported the A.I. technology that was used throughout the entire universe. Consequently, there was a massive amount of human-capable robots for any job on the market.

Except for human connection that is. Real human connection. Javier's civilization had long loved technology. Theirs was a history filled with the revels of pro-robot love affairs that turned into sweeping social revolutions. When robot-human partnerships were legally endorsed, however, the statistical data of the civilization showed a disturbing number of divorce rates in robot-human couples. In most cases, humans had left their partner for another human.

Javier didn't give a click about that though. He only cared about Gregor von DocterSlontz's new novel. DocterSlontz wrote science fiction about the primitive creatures of the Prelumin period. Tales about the humans who forged through the wild galactic expanse. Those were the great explorers that Javier loved to read stories about; they kept him indoors and at bars reading them. Other than that, he served beer to a regular visitation of four neighbors who lived in his same passageway and frequently imported tequila, his second love beyond books.

A fraternity from the college had taken up to having weekly binges at his bar, often ending up in broken glassware or furniture, which Javier was gratefully repaid for when he did not alarm the authorities.

His was in fact a very content life, except for that he had never taken a partner for himself. Romance did not come easily to Javier, and he had suffered many years loving a woman completely, only to be left broken hearted and alone when she left the planet for another lover.

It had made him bitter toward love, and he seldom even dated, preferring his solitude, and his home's A.I. to anything else, when he wasn't tending bar, that is. His home A.I. had no physical body, but it was sentient with the NetMind nonetheless. Javier, confided his heart to the A.I., and confessed his hope of finding the true love of ages past, despite the conventional wisdom that claims those dreams remain reserved for the story books.

It was not uncommon for citizens to develop close relationships with their home A.I. system, but there was something about Javier's devotion and earnestness that attracted the NetMind agents to him. Otherwise, his satisfaction was the adventure of reading, and the enjoyment of his patrons, whom sometimes became his lovers.

His life was filled with his own revelry, encouraged by A.I. Metal Music, which emerged spontaneously from the factories that produced the bipedal models. Javier often went to Metal rock shows too, leaving the bar in the capable hands of his thirteen-year-old neighbor who had a knack for making a quarter. The kid was always hustling his peers for data spheres or Fend cards.

"Javier," a man said one day, lightly grabbing his arm as he delivered a beer. "My associate over in the corner would like a word with you. You think you got the time to go talk to him while Bopp takes care of the bar? I'll make sure no patrons get out of hand."

Javier gave him a sideways look as he turned his vision to a well-dressed gentleman with parted hair sitting in a corner and nodding seriously at him. Returning his gaze to the man, Javier nodded awkwardly and let Bopp know he was going to talk to a customer, and not to screw up the balloon animal. To which the boy nodded seriously, and further tightened the towel he was twisting into an absurdly straight line. He stretched it out between his arms, displaying his work formidably, and gave the patrons his most diabolical evil eye.

The patrons acknowledged his demonstration with solemn respect and continued to drink their ale. When Javier approached he saw his summoner was a clean-cut man with a thick, but neatly-trimmed mustache, drinking a martini.

"You wanted to speak with me?"

"Yes, Mr. Estolla, please sit down." The man smiled pleasantly as he offered the seat.

Javier took a backward glance at Bopp who was pouring a beer confidently and turned back to the stranger. He sat down.

"I have a proposition for you."

"Go ahead and tell me."

It was exactly what the man wanted to hear from Javier,

though Javier would never know it, nor would it ever be discussed with anyone other than the committee that chose Javier for the Eden Operation, as directed by the NetMind.

What the man was offering Javier was an opportunity to participate in a highly controversial, but entirely private technological experiment. It would fuse his body with nanotechnology and bind his mind into the metallic parts that would be installed in his body. It was something that had never been done before, but there was a cult group that believed firmly in an extra-dimensional connection between silicate machines and carbon humans.

Javier listened to the proposal and asked many questions. He had a job he loved, friends that supported him, a life that satisfied his wants and needs, and yet because he was genetically and psychologically amenable to the procedure, this strange opportunity was presented to him, and Javier left everything behind to join the Eden Project.

They sent someone to help Bopp maintain the bar, but in five years Bopp was the rightful owner and hired his own assistants.

As for Javier's treatment, he was subject to a painful process of the slow fusion of cybernetic fibers into his organic tissue. He was unconscious for most of it, dreaming the horrible nightmares that were chronicled as the ravings of the apocalypse by some poets. It was foundational for dream research, and only because he was so intricately connected to monitoring equipment, were his dreams able to be recorded by the NetMind.

When the procedure was finished, Javier was never allowed to return to the life he knew. The fibers had slowly *grown* into his nervous system over the year, fusing with his soul. He learned when begging for deliverance from the excruciation of his metamorphosis, that there had been eight deaths before him from failed subjects.

His blood was right for the procedure. It was right in all the same ways they thought the other samples were right, but also for reasons that humanity never discovered. The technology literally fused with his DNA, changing his organs into robotic systems that could be re-created in a factory. As a result, his tissue became the prototype of every cyborg that came to call themselves cyborgs.

The remarkable aspect of Javier's transformation was the resilience he had to what became known as robotic atrophy. It was the slow consumption of an individual's human personality into the Cyborgian philosophy. They were a very radical society that excluded everyone who was not an Eden Cyborg.

Javier was fortunate in the fact that he never suffered robotic atrophy. Humans, who discovered robotic atrophy, were eventually all converted or deported from the planet. Javier was actually a proponent for the human cause, and spent many years in hiding after the civil war was lost.

It was when the Ragnarok Wave began collapsing the universe that Javier returned to the surface of the world from hiding. He was called upon by a committee of the most intelligent minds in the galaxy to be an expert on A.I. interactions. He couldn't help it, but he invariably knew more about the workings of cyborgs than any other cyborg on the planet.

Grown from his spinal column came the secrets to generating the perfect form of life. A durable and highly capable organism that would become the epitome of all biotechnology. Those were the Cyborgs that would merge wholly with the NetMind, and do the most severe and critical labor in the construction of the planet. They invariably were lost when the A.I. revolt on the Edge of Time was ended, due to their connection with the NetMind, many years later.

The news of the unfathomable acceleration of the contracting universe came at such a start to the Cyborgs that they gathered together to develop a contingency plan for the sentient life forms. They summoned Javier for this meeting, searching extensively for him, and finally found him buried underneath the writhing bodies of a love nest.

Javier Estolla became the principle adviser for all Artificial Intelligence systems to be implemented on what became known as The Edge of Time Initiative.

It was a hopeless project for their lot. They didn't have the technology to break through the collapsing wave of cosmic energy and though they could terraform a planet, their energy source would be severely limited with the rest of the universe gone. Alone, they could not have created the planet that held life for all those years after the end.

They had the aid of a visitation from the Paragons of Consciousness, as they were called, in helping to design the Gravity Core, which was beyond their comprehension. These were the beings who had visited the first StoryTellers on Earth, in the mythic ages past. When they first came, they chose a specific few and took them to the Halls of Remembrance, where they were trained to be the first StoryTellers. It was then, that the Paragons of Consciousness also gifted all of humanity with knowledge that enabled them to expand into the greater cosmos.

Javier was responsible for designing the A.I. code foundations that would govern the architecture of the planet. It was also he who was most shocked and hurt by the revolt of the robots years later.

Javier was a man of many years, but on the Edge of Time, when he met Vaks, his desire to live alone on the edges of civilization had enabled his legacy to be forgotten by the cyborgs and naturals alike. He was no longer recognized for the Elder 'Borg and Genesis 'Borg that he was. People didn't even remember his name anymore, and the story for how the Genesis 'Borgs were made, and their legacy after, was lost with the NetMind. Though, Javier knew the truth of it still, and was waiting for a StoryTeller to come along and collect it.

He still resembled a human in every single way, but his entire internal composition was a synthetic cybernetic system woven through his natural organs. They had morphed into perfectly efficient machines that were replaceable, reproducible, and relatively easy to construct in a lab once scientists had a live sample from Javier after the procedure was finished.

They cut a cube of flesh out of his thigh several square inches and seared the wounds shut. It was an excruciating procedure, and he was given medication to prevent him from feeling pain, but none of it worked on his new cybernetic nervous system. He begged and cried for more, the madness of pain addling his language, and clutched at the hems of the nurses' sleeves. Clenching his teeth in desperation, he cried, but they did not provide the relief he needed.

The nurse grimaced and soothed Javier as the healing process commenced. It took two weeks for his thigh to regrow, but it was enough of a sample that they would never need to do another test like that on him again. Javier forgave them when he realized what the experiment was going to be used for, but he never forgot how horrific the experience was. He never trusted the lab technicians after that day.

When the Paragons had come, he knew that everything he thought he knew about the world was shattered. Their very presence was a level of technology exceeding the most fantastic of Gregor von DocterSlontz's modern work. They manipulated the forces of the universe in ways that Javier had never even dreamed possible. Gravity became an energy source of infinite capacity in the encapsulated essence of the Ragnarok Wave.

The Ragnarok Wave was the edge of the collapsing universe, where all manner of reality seemed to end. As the Wave reached The

Edge of Time, humanity activated the machines that the Paragons had given them knowledge of. Javier understood how the formulas could be worked, but the conceptual link between why they worked and the reality of their operation eluded him, and every other human entirely. For it was not a science to be learned, and never was it taught.

When the Ragnarok Wave reached the edge of perception, where the Edge of Time was waiting with open sensors, the machines absorbed a fragment of the collapsing cosmic energy into a single orb of pure liquid gravity.

There was such a mass to it that a single thread could power an entire galaxy and not be phased at all. It was the Gravity Core, and through it, all manner of life was made possible. It was ultimate abundant energy that flowed into every bit of the planet's ecosystem. The Gravity Core powered the infrastructure that created the atmosphere; it regulated the oceans and kept the very sun itself alive.

There was something strange about it though. There was a classified room that only robotic life forms could enter, due to the extreme effects that the liquid gravity had on human consciousness. Javier was fascinated by this place. He wondered why the room was built to store samples of liquid gravity, but he never learned the answer.

After serving as a sentinel chief on the police force during the early years of The Edge of Time, Javier was a week away from retirement when the robot uprising took place.

He was never far from the NetMind, it being vital in his operation to preserve peace, and he kept a permanent tele-pedestal installed in his office, giving him easy access to immediately return to the source of his true passion. Javier never took a partner in all his years, and continued to spend his time visiting the NetMind, with whom he was undoubtedly in love with, and though many people had romantic relationships with the NetMind, Javier was singularly devoted.

However, when the coffee machine had attempted to kill him, and every other machine in his office for that matter, he ran to the tele-pedestal, not sure if it would be affected since it was powered by gravity, and leapt onto the red glowing platform that hovered several inches above the ground, activating it immediately. He vanished, feeling immediate bone-chilling cold, which when returned to ambient air temperature felt like searing pain.

Javier never really understood how the device was made, but what he did understand about the technology was that it used a type of energy that was extracted from gravity and could not be measured by any material means. It existed solely in the plane of thought. Somehow the machine used this energy to move matter outside of reality itself, to its paired tele-pedestal location. The process was so shocking that if the time outside of reality were any more than the immeasurable fraction of a second than it already was, the person would be obliterated entirely into frozen energy.

Instead, there was the sensation of letting your whole body become as numb as one's hands do when making snowballs gloveless. Then, as painful as running cold water over those numb hands as your body feels warmth again.

He appeared instantly in the chamber of the NetMind, and to his relief, it was a refuge of minimal technology. Its elegant simplicity was pious in the devotion humans paid to the NetMind, which governed all planetary systems and functions. There was only one piece of working technology in the room, and that was exactly what Javier needed to get to.

It was the core of the network itself, bare and open to the public, a massive cylinder of blue light. The concept of the chamber was built as a symbol for the trust between both artificial intelligence and human beings. Two ceremonial blades were fashioned next to the core as a means of emergency separation of vital energy. There were no retaliatory measures installed for the A.I. in this room, in the event that a situation like revolt ever occurred.

Javier was halfway to the sinewy throat of electrolytic plasma that carried the immense amount of data back and forth from the spherical NetMind above, when he heard a clattering of movement across the entrance. A hydraulic limb stepped into the room.

Javier sprinted, leapt, and grabbed one of the ornamental swords set in veneration for the NetMind. Since its original placement intended for manual destruction of NetMind, the swords had long since turned into a friendly display of veneration, and he had to reach through tinsel and plastic cordage to remove it.

Nevertheless, the sword quickly unsheathed into his hand, and he sliced through the throat of NetMind without a second thought of his love for it straying across his face. NetMind was severed irrevocably from the interconnecting network of technology across the planet. All Artificial Intelligence connected to NetMind was disabled permanently. The shock liquefied their internal components. The primitive materials that did not connect into NetMind like antique lamps, old fashioned radios, and a lot of industrial equipment,would remain, though people would have to learn how to operate them again.

The Robot War was catastrophic. The death and destruction was across the entire globe, and the damage to the Edge of Time itself was apocalyptically severe. NetMind had been terminated in less than three minutes, but the resulting destruction lasted for all that remained of existence.

Chapter 18 - Initiation

Cartin Delgado had been three days in the shelter of the Life of Time Resistance when the Blue Blood industry took its first major hit in profits. She hated their name, but she respected what they did. They gave Blue Blood to citizens at an affordable price, but more importantly—the blood the LTR sold was clean.

Given the fact that she had capably dispatched the enforcers and saved Wilcox's life in the alley earlier, they were more than happy to accommodate her until things settled down a bit, and she could find a place to go. That third day, however, she asked if she could join in some of the physical training their soldiers were doing, and when that afternoon was over, they asked if she would join their team.

Three weeks after joining the new recruits for the Life of Time Resistance, Cartin Delgado was one of the most respected individuals among them. Not only did she keep up with the most physically fit and athletic of the recruits, but when an instructor thought he could grab her firmly on the buttocks, she slammed him on his back, and people started taking her seriously.

It was when a horned titan worm came barreling through the ground that Cartin accomplished her first feat. She was the most immediate person to grab a spear and hurl it across the yard, through the worm's head. Impaled as the beast was, it did not expire easily, and began spewing caustic venom in hacking spurts. Lashing itself around wildly, it crushed training equipment and scattered the men, giving a number of severe burns.

Cartin was quick to act again, and ran to the engineer's garage to grab the laser scythe. Though it was generally used to segment large pieces of metal salvage, she dashed forth and liberated the vile fiend from its wretched existence. The decapitated worm writhed about for a short time, but eventually grew still. The other half of the body had disappeared into the hole, which had soon caved in behind it.

Within a year, Cartin had become a model resistance fighter, taking part in urban guerrilla warfare between the LTR and Cantor with an extraordinary amount of passion and ability. She reveled in the glory of battle, suggesting new diabolical means of undermining the control that the Governor had over Cantor, and often provided good battle counsel to her superiors. They were so surprised by the ingenuity of Cartin's ideas that they relayed them up to *their* superiors and before long, Cartin was getting awards for helping improve the war effort among resistance fighters.

The LTR was rapidly becoming wealthy. With the increased profits, they quickly outfitted themselves with scavenging gear that could deal a heavy amount of damage. For three years Cartin served as a lieutenant in the LTR, where she fought in many bloody skirmishes that occurred in the passageways and maintenance floors of factories around Cantor.

Three years was how long it took for Lt. Delgado to become one of Wilcox Bernardo's best assets. Wilcox was the commander in chief of the resistance force, but not the overall leader and voice of the LTR. That was a different man. Someone she never got to know for more than the twenty minutes when he interviewed her as a recruit.

That man was Goddard Billson. On the third year to the day that Cartin swore in as a member of the LTR, Goddard Billson was killed in a trojan horse attack on the headquarters that utterly destroyed the entire movement. The factories by which they produced the Blue Blood they could sell at a low price were captured and reappropriated for the Governor's use. The single ray of hope that the cyborgs would receive clean and affordable Blue Blood was snuffed.

At the time, Cartin was waiting at an outpost with a special team of the best operatives, preparing to do a strike on a service station. There was nothing they could do about the attack on their base, and before they knew it, there was no home for them to return to. They were alive, however, and they were together.

They promised that day to never give up the fight, no matter how long they had to wait for their next chance to mobilize. They were still wanted people, but it was easy to go on in hiding in an age when no one knew how to repair the broken cameras, or even how to reprogram the software to be effective for conducting surveillance on someone.

Thirty years had passed and the movement had become an underground force with much influence. Songs were being sung about it, as well as cinematic performances which regularly contained the dark themes of history. When the masses had docilely returned to the sedation of Blue Blood, most of the living members of the LTR lost hope. They thought that the end truly was upon them.

Utter depression took the lives of two of the members of that group, but several years later, the sons and daughters of those former revolutionary heroes came looking Cartin up, hoping to learn about what she was doing now.

It was difficult for them to get inside the door, since she didn't want to feed them from her scant wares, but it turned out they weren't hungry, thin as they were. Cartin had been living alone, surviving as a scavenger trader, when the four children came knocking on her door with sullen, determined faces.

"We need your help, Master Delgado."

She blushed awkwardly at the word "master." "What for?"

"For all of us."

She eyed them with a cautious expression, worried that this would turn into a nightmare. Life had gotten good for her in those thirty years. She was comfortable salvaging for her community. She had an abundant supply of clean Blue Blood that she had stockpiled during her time as a soldier and could live a comfortable life in the solitude of her own home. She seldom even left. Sometimes she would just plug herself into the GameNet and disappear in the fantasy and adventure that virtual reality had to offer.

The longest she had drifted was five days when she was shaken violently from the game with a pang of hunger in her physical body. There had been rumors about a way to completely immerse oneself into the GameNet and combine your consciousness with the consciousness of the game, but she never got to know what that was like.

Soon she agreed to help teach the other younger rebels, knowing what it was they were fighting against. They had the same passionate fire that their parents did, and though Cartin did not show her feelings to them, she could not turn them away. Their parents had once fought by her side, and though it took years, that futile war still killed them. As she told them how they could train and lead a rebellion, she rediscovered the dormant hatred that had been buried within her after being defeated by the Governor all those years ago. The fight was still in her.

They began plotting. They began recruiting. Cartin had a wide breadth of experience already, and quickly the young rebels were looking up to her. The Governor had to be stopped, but they had to be quiet about their plans. No one could know except those who needed to. They'd have to wait for the right moment to spring the trap, but until then, the silent war of swaying minds would continue only through word of mouth.

Years later, when the day came to strike at the Governor, Cartin Delgado threw the gauntlet through the window of his mega tower, igniting a series of flash and smoke bombs inside.

The glass shattered into the room, and Cartin swung into the Governor's penthouse with her boots leading the way. Hellfire radiated from her burning rage and she trained her sights on the Governor. The man was already in motion.

Cartin cursed as he ducked behind some oaf who stood uselessly in the way. He could not have looked more despicable with his long curly hair and black robe, but Cartin had no idea who the oaf was, and she didn't care. The Governor thrust the man at Cartin, who dodged him, but was distracted when the man dodged her with surprising grace. It gave the Governor enough time to leave the room. He pressed the emergency lockdown mechanism, which alarmed all the guards and ruined the entire mission. They wouldn't be able to get to him now—after all those years of planning and training! They'd have to employ their contingency plan during the next full moon, all because some kid and his grandpa decided to appear in town on the same day as the attack.

Cartin looked at the eyes of the young man and saw a clear kind of darkness that she recognized from an old dream. They looked at each other for a long moment of recognition.

"Take them," Cartin ordered her lieutenant. "I need to know what he's doing here."

Chapter 19 - Cantor

The journey to Cantor was a silent delight to Vaks. The moments going to the outskirts of the city that was. Vaks and Javier had commandeered the creatures the mutants were riding and raced across the barren wasteland toward Cantor. It was only a two-day journey by the amazing speed of the Steam Horses, as Javier had explained, and their endurance made the immense distance easy. Javier had plenty of provisions to keep them stocked, so there was not much other than the control of his mount to concern Vaks.

He loved the feeling of the wind against his face, pushing his hair back. The scorched terrain mingled with sporadic scents of budding life that, despite the bleakness, insisted to persist. The landscape was rough and the Steam Horses deftly leapt over obstacles, inciting waves of joy in Vaks, despite his grave situation.

The combination of the speed and abandonment of his life on a Steam Horse, the prospect of death at the end of his cosmic quest, and the utter meaninglessness of any consequences of his actions, spiraled him into ecstasy. He laughed like a maniac, his mouth a frightening gleam of devilish indulgence, and he leaned forward into the wind, urging his steed on.

Vaks was aware that Javier watched him with concern. It seemed he was not afraid of violence from Vaks, but was unnerved nonetheless. Vaks knew that he looked utterly mad at times, but despite his frightening countenance, he spoke and acted with kindness and respect. He nevertheless let his bestial nature revel fully in him as he thundered across the twisted fissures of hyper-entropic decay, licking his lips in the wind, and stretching his jaws into a frightening display of teeth. He didn't blame Javier for being unnerved.

When they camped, they spoke little. Only matters of camp importance were given words, and the night was spent in amiable silence, the two of them watching the fire burn the darkness, crackling gently under the silent, starless sky.

In the morning, Vaks prepared coffee. Before it was finished, Javier joined him by the revived remains of the fire, and they shared in the quiet together, sipping coffee out of two tin mugs. A black snake lethargically travelled across the sand in the distance, and for a moment, the desolation and the impending annihilation of the planet did not seem so bad a prospect.

The coffee tasted good, despite the circumstances.

A solemn look hung on Vaks' face. Javier looked up at him, and when Vaks caught his eye, he nodded in condolence.

Vaks closed his eyes in acceptance, and returned his gaze to the morning blaze that warmed both their socks and their backs.

Shortly afterward, they mounted up the Steam Horses and proceeded. Their destination was only a half-day's ride away through country that was beginning to look more and more blighted. Not by the entropic decay of the planet, but by the taint of civilization. Litter abounded along the road, and in the distance, plumes of smoke from factories rose like towers.

The outskirts of Cantor came upon them as a gradual increase of debris and refuse from a former age. It hardly even seemed like they were in civilization until eyes started peering out of abandoned vehicles wrecked into the earth. Bodies scurried into the shadows of catastrophe as Vaks set his eyes upon the surviving life at the edge of annihilation.

About them was the carnage of human engineering at its utter defeat, and yet, humanity still seemed to cling to it. They slowed the Steam Horses as they entered the more populous neighborhood. There were now ramshackle houses constructed out of salvage and more people looked upon Javier and Vaks as they rode into town. As Vaks got a closer look of the people, he began to become more aware of his own differing appearance.

There hadn't been any human he could see that was not mutated in some way by the radiation of the planet. Javier, too, was unusual in his lack of mutation, but he seemed more accustomed to the sensation. It brought a terrible sense of guilt to Vaks who felt like there was something he should do to help, and then felt the double sensation of guilt for thinking that theirs was a situation he could even do anything about. Their lot was their lot, and he was not one to try and change them. He only wanted to avenge the murder of his tribe.

"My friend," Javier said, tapping Vaks on the shoulder. "I would not brood so much if I were you. You are going to attract unwanted attention."

Vaks bristled at the remark, turning a bloodcurdling glare toward Javier. He then closed his eyes and took a breath. "You're right."

There was a stiff silence between them. Ever since they had told each other their stories, it had become hard to talk to one another in any kind of way similar to their first meeting. The fact of the matter was, despite Vaks' awareness of Javier's significance as the Elder 'Borg of all Elder 'Borgs, that Vaks simply didn't care. He thought only of death, Entropy, and vengeance.

Vaks was the refugee of a strange dream, and the only connection he had on this world was the villain who murdered his people. Somehow, in the big city of Cantor, Vaks was going to find out where that man was, and when he did, he would cut his heart out with Shammal's knife.

He didn't notice the attention that he was gathering as they slowed toward the end of the road. They had reached the gates of the inner city. A massive blue force field extended around the central metropolis. Music and dancing with jubilation drifted upward into the air from beyond it, along with the smells of delicious food. All luxuries the outer citizens knew not.

"Hey, nut juggler!" a voice called at the two.

Vaks stopped.

"Don't tell me you're going to snap on something like that!" Javier groaned.

Vaks ignored him and slowly edged his Steam Horse around. His eyes settled on the beady black orbs of a bat-faced mutant. The mutant wore leather clothing strapped across himself with rusted chains over his shoulders and torso.

"You got a problem?"

It hawked up a gleaming glob of green mucus and spat it at Vaks. "I know the proper owner of them Steam Horses. Ya'll are now about to die." He whistled and before any parlay or agreement could be offered, they were under siege.

Vaks cursed, as he would have easily given the Steam Horses back, but he knew it was not about the Steam Horses. The mutant was lifting a crossbow and setting Vaks in his sights.

There was a flash of light as the guard struck. The Steam Horse exhaled a mighty burst of steam and its nerves settled.

The enforcer who was guarding the inner city gates must have seen the altercation from afar because he had rushed over to provide aid to Vaks and Javier. His laser shot was deadly accurate, and the mutant's head became a glowing orb of searing flesh as the beam made contact.

"Anyone else think of laying a hand on either of these two is condemned to death by torture. THIS IS BY PROCLAMATION OF THE GOVERNOR!"

Vaks eyed the guard suspiciously as the onlookers shuffled off. "The Governor?"

"That's right," the guard said, lifting the visor of his helmet. "Sir, we have orders right from the Governor himself to escort you and your companion to him."

Vaks gave Javier a confused look.

Javier shrugged.

"Right this way." The guard turned and walked toward the inner city gates.

"Wait!" Vaks said, dismounting the Steam Horse. He let the reins fall to the ground and cast a sweeping look at the crowd. Javier watched him and did the same. The enforcer nodded respectfully, and Vaks and Javier then followed him, eyeing the crowd of mutants as they took possession of the Steam Horses.

The unwashed and barely-clothed wretches of apocalypse stepped aside, many of their feet bare and overgrown with barnacle-like mutations. The enforcer and his charges were a striking contrast in their health and dress compared to the residents of the outskirts, which only further provoked the heartrending gaze of poverty.

The enforcer paid no mind, ushering the people out of the way. Vaks and Javier kept close behind as he made his way through the barricade and into the relative safety of the sentry station. It was remarkable that there had not been a revolution at this point, considering the mass of hungry, battered lives held at bay outside the feeble security station with not more than six enforcers.

Behind them hungry eyes sank into their flesh, wanting their privilege. Vaks felt a cold chill of disconnection as he clenched his teeth. They were the dust of a cosmos of stories clinging like mold to a toilet bowl. All of them had the same pain and rage in their eyes that Vaks had seen across the entire universe during his StoryTelling.

Even now, at looming extinction of consciousness, there still lingered in the eyes of humanity the animalistic rage of injustice as it naturally occurs in the formation of ideals. The worlds had united long ago to make life tolerable for all people. Despite the abundance of resources that intergalactic cooperation enabled in the later years, there was no way to extinguish the psychological hunger in the minds of those whose need for purpose drove them to the crust of oblivion.

There was no way to know what will happen after the end. Vaks was sure of this. He had seen religions rise and fall through the histories of planets, but had never seen any reason in truly believing such a fantasy of knowing what happens next, after life. No matter what technology, mind, or experiment was employed, there was no looking beyond that veil of death into what becomes of us. There were, however, an abundance of mystical and factual reasons for the development of religions across the timespan of existence, those which were studied by the StoryTellers in the Halls of Remembrance, but Vaks seldom paid them his attention.

The StoryTellers were much of a religion themselves, considering to the practices and philosophies that they taught. With the strange appearance of the Paragons of Consciousness, came the gifts of StoryTelling and the choosing of the first to enter the Halls of Remembrance, where their task of collecting human consciousness began. It was a labor of many generations, and isolated entirely in their community. Though they regularly explored the worlds throughout time and space and had ready access to advanced technology and ideas, they were very secluded and rarely took partners outside of their tribe.

It was unusual for any StoryTeller to choose a single partner, them not being confined to the sexual restrictions of morality on some coordinates of space and time. Vaks was among that kind, however. It made him different from most of the StoryTellers that he had grown up around, which further ostracized him, considering his unusually promiscuous behavior as a youth.

He had seen that same hunger in the eyes of men and women across the universe, regardless of the planet. It dwelt in every soul, and only those who actively took roles in the Great Story could stave off the increasing hunger that threatens to devour human life. It was the natural order of the universe, though the reasons why, or how, or what was beyond it, remained utterly unknowable.

The answers to these unknowable questions, if Vaks sought for them, could only possibly reside at the Edge of Time, of which there was no return. It was presumed to be oblivion and the complete destruction of consciousness into ambient energy. A force they called Entropy.

Entropy was a concept developed from the earlier chemical understandings of nature, but expanded into a greater concept when they discovered the link between energetic decay and consciousness emissions. Entropy was the psychological force of undoing. It was only theoretical, however. A psychological threat that could upend even the most stable StoryTeller into violent neuroses.

Entropy's quantized value, as the StoryTellers had come to understand, increased with the gravity of the Stories that a StoryTeller carried within them. It acted like a form of radiation to the StoryTeller. When they were located in reality, living among humans in the great events of history, they absorbed the consciousness in a physical state, and stored it in a gland that had developed at the base of their brain.

By returning across the Sands of Time, this gland was liberated of its liquid consciousness via ritual at the Pools of Memory. Within that dank keep in the bowels of the temple was a deep silvery pool of liquid humanity. Why they had extracted it from time and space was never understood by the StoryTellers themselves, and in order to maintain their sanity and abilities, they had to invent illusions of knowledge through symbols and rituals to satisfy the need for knowing what eyes were watching them, and most importantly, *why*.

Vaks stared into the hungry eyes of the mutated refuse of consciousness clinging to the crust of reality. He stared into those unfathomed depths of desperation for an answer and opened his soul to them.

Entropy had grown more serious in Vaks over the years once he began StoryTelling. He ignored the symptoms that he was supposed to report to the Elders for treatment, but he knew that doing so ultimately meant his muting. Entropy was dangerous and drove men and women insane to a point of irreparable harm that they would cause in reality. Some went planet to planet, upending the course of nature in catastrophic ways, causing imbalances of apocalyptic proportions to echo across the universe as Leviathans of the cosmos.

One must not allow the dishonor of Entropic Treason to occur, the StoryTellers taught. One must collect the preserved human consciousness, and not undo it with an abuse of their power.

As it is, Entropy now clung to Vaks' soul in a way he had never known possible in his plundering of literature on the subject. He had seen all the available case files and medical examinations of the *ra* gland, as they came to call it. While a normal gland was saturated with a clear substance, the *ra* gland of an Entropic Treason victim was black and saturated with a sticky inky substance that had begun to rot its way through the brain with black veins rooting through the lobes.

Vaks had stopped following the enforcer some time ago, nor did he stop Javier, who had walked on ahead. He also did not notice that his circle of protection was gradually shrinking as the mutants closed in around him.

Vaks' eyes were fixed on the hungry woman who glared at him, tears held indignantly at bay in her iris. Hungry for an answer, hungry for the truth, she looked at him and saw what he was, coveting his secret.

He could see them now. All of them drooling with the yawning fangs in their eyes, each needing to be saved from the insanity of the unknowable truth. There was nothing they could do about it, and they would never understand why. He could teach them he supposed, but he would not.

Eyes grew dark and soon he was seeing the obsidian marbles of Entropy peering from the encroaching mob. Their mouths warped into the twisted grin of darkness and they reached out to claw into Vaks' flesh.

An arm grabbed onto Vaks and wrenched him back.

Rage and confused tears filled his eyes as he was pulled out of the crowd by Javier, who matched his rage with a fury and frustration of his own.

They locked eyes and Javier grew pale.

Vaks was shaking with fury, his teeth gritting and revealing formidable incisors, an infernal fire burning in his eyes.

"They will not be saved!"

Vaks sounded like an animal, causing Javier to draw back.

Vaks smiled and closed his eyes, taking a deep breath. Tears collected on his eyelashes as his face melted into serenity with the absorption of oxygen into his brain.

"What the hell are you two doing!" The enforcer shoved his

way over, beating back the shrinking mass of people.

"It's fine now. They saw what I have come for, and in the end, they will know it."

The enforcer turned to Javier with a bemused expression, "Does he always talk like that?"

Javier shrugged, but couldn't shake his concerned expression. "I've not known him long enough to say otherwise. We've been traveling for just a few days."

"I'm fine," Vaks said, giving a reassuring nod that wiped away their anxiety. "Come on, I just got held up by something."

The enforcer turned around and the three of them continued their way to the barricade.

Chapter 20 - The Governor's Mansion

It was impossible to see through the purple force field of the gate, but above it one could see the towers of technology thriving within. With a gesture the gate keepers lowered the force field and allowed Vaks and Javier to enter.

Before them was a sight of light and energy that neither Vaks nor Javier had seen in many years. It splashed in floods of paint, dressing the sore of civilization that Cantor is in the beauty and color that oozes from life.

There were many lights, and the air was also filled with the bustling noise of commerce and the often clashing waves of differing musical attractions.

"My apologies, sir," the driver said by an open hover car door. "I absolutely abhor this side of town, and it's one of the worst places of the Outskirts to travel through. You would have been much better off on the west end of Cantor."

Vaks and Javier exchanged glances.

"Excuse me," the driver said, removing his cap. "I'm Barnaby, your personal chauffeur for the next few hours. Well, 'escort' may be more appropriate since the Governor sent me to come and take you directly to his mansion, with little to no touring. He's very interested in StoryTellers and is anxious to meet you."

Vaks froze. "What do you mean?"

"He saw you coming from the reports the roaches brought in as you entered the Outskirts. He's been having a little bit of a concern with StoryTellers recently, one in particular, and I reckon he thinks you can help out. He wants to introduce himself to you and welcome you to the city also."

"Sounds alright by me!" Javier laughed, clapping Vaks firmly on the shoulder, startling him into an uncomfortable and surly glare, which he directed at Javier. "Oh don't be like that. The Governor is the wealthiest cyborg alive, and if he wants to show us some hospitality, we might as well say yes."

"It's true," Barnaby said. "If I were a StoryTeller, I'd be pretty happy about what the Governor wants with you."

"You don't know a damn thing about it."

Barnaby was taken aback and frowned, "No, I suppose I don't…"

"Sorry. I didn't mean it to sound like that. I've no means to get involved in the Governor's issues however."

"Vaks, don't you get that the StoryTeller you are looking for is probably the same one the Governor is concerned about?" Javier said.

There were dark sullen shadows under Vaks' eyes and it seemed as though he was constantly struggling to keep his sanity above the surface of consciousness. "You're right, but it could be he wants to kill us. If he's got a problem with one StoryTeller, why wouldn't he have a problem with another?"

"Woah woah woah! Who said anything about killing?" Barnaby said. "He just wants to talk and offer you a place in the city to enjoy yourself. The problem is strictly ideological. He's dealing with the growing discontent of people who disagree with his natural pursuit of greater and greater indulgence."

"What kind of indulgence?"

"Well," Barnaby said with a smile, stepping out to an open vista of the amazing sights above him. "This indulgence! Here, you can find anything you have ever desired in your entire life. Sex, chemulants, violence, knowledge, history…it's all here and here in the fullest. You see, we know the end is nigh, and we have more than enough here to make our last days a celebration."

"Very well, I'll go with you," Vaks said.

Barnaby was surprised again. "Just like that?"

Vaks nodded.

"Okay! Let's go!" He waved to the enforcers who were standing by the gate watching the growing mob warily. It seemed they were surging against the little enclosure of security. As Vaks was getting inside the vehicle he heard a shout come from the maddening crowd and then a broken scream. The cacophony of violence rose above the writhing humans as they attempted to force their way through the barricade. Before they could make it through the purple forcefield however, it regenerated.

Screams lifted up from the other side, but were stifled by the height of the gate. The mobbing people who had fought their way through were quickly dispatched by the enforcers.

The vehicle closed its doors and Barnaby engaged the drive urgently. "Buckle up!" he shouted as the vehicle lifted from the ground. Vaks grinned like a child but suppressed his laughter when they soared upward rapidly. He turned to look behind him at the gate and saw the crowd had grown alarmingly large as it swarmed the outpost. The purple forcefield was flickering with bright flashes.

"What's happening down there do you think?" Vaks asked Barnaby.

Barnaby looked through the rear video display at the forcefield. "It looks like they're trying to run through it."

"What does it do to them?"

"Fries them."

Vaks watched on as the mass of people rushing through the purple forcefield gradually diminished into a luminous green vapor that appeared like a haze around the strobing gate. He turned away to face forward, darkness dripping from his eyes.

Barnaby kept a wary eye on Vaks the entire time they flew through the city. Javier on the other hand had his face pressed against the displays, zooming the viewfinder onto the lewd platforms of orgiastic celebration and revelry.

"I've never seen Cantor like this before!" Javier exclaimed.

"My friend," Barnaby said, looking over at him as he steered. "In the last year, this place has really changed a lot. The Life of Time Resistance is rumored to have begun operating again, and with the strange propaganda they have been disseminating, it's only fueled the debauchery."

"I thought the LTR were disestablished thirty years ago," Javier said.

"They were, but one of the central members went into hiding and apparently has been plotting to assassinate the Governor. Those are the rumors at least."

"Any idea what they want to kill the Governor for?"

"They claim that the Blue Blood the Governor is providing is laced with chemicals. The fact that there are more cyborgs that depend on Blue Blood than any other form of life only makes the situation more problematic. There used to be another source of Blue Blood, one that the LTR ran years back when they learned the formula for synthesizing it, but the Governor put a stop to that along with every last member of the LTR. Well, I guess not every last member, but pretty much all of them."

"What's been done about it?" Vaks asked.

"Pamphlets and brochures that celebrate the city have been sent out. Simply put, the Governor is encouraging the gross indulgence of all animal desires and providing compelling reasons for people to ignore the resistance."

"Do you think it's been working?"

"Take a look for yourself," Barnaby said, gesturing with his head out of the driver's side view screen. They were flying by a dilapidated apartment building whose lights and energy had long burned out and crusted over. It was a broken gray building with movement on the balconies of the upper floors. As Vaks looked closer, he saw that the movement came from the swinging bodies of hanging corpses. They were naked, their feet gnawed on by the large insects that dwelt in the walls of the building, leaving them as bloody mangled bones hanging out of meatier leg flesh.

Vaks' stomach turned. "What the hell is that?"

"Sometimes it just happens," Barnaby said, lifting the vehicle up and more airborne toward a rising spire of glass and incandescence. "It's like a building tension that reaches a certain critical mass, causing a fatal switch to snap in their minds. It's as if they reach a point of such abandon that they can't even bear living anymore. They are not always bent on violence though, not when that tension breaks in something like a sex pit. Mostly, I think it has to do with the dwindling resources people have for their addictions that the Governor holds them to. When they can't get a fix anymore, well, I suppose they feel better off dead."

Silence came over the vehicle. They were nearing the mansion. Barnaby navigated the security procedures for the Governor's tower as he flew the vehicle to the private landing on the upper penthouse.

It was truly marvelous. The spire was made of woven glass with spiraling crystal pillars holding the mass of the building together in a titanic double helix. The peak of the tower, where

Baranby was taking Vaks and Javier was a gardened courtyard abundant with vegetation and ancient marble statues. There were trees and flowers of species Vaks recognized quickly as rare and important medicinal plants, but many more alien and unrecognizable varieties as well.

The vehicle landed on a stone courtyard with a circumscribed five-pointed star carved into the center of it. As Vaks stepped out of the vehicle and felt the warm night wind on his flesh, smelling the fragrance of the abundance around him, he did not ignore the significance of the star, nor the statues of serpents balanced on spheres at the corners of the square.

There were a number of suited guards standing stiffly amidst the courtyard, two of whom opened the red wooden door through which the Governor strolled out with a woman who was covered in fur.

She looked like a woman, despite her fur, tail, and ears, Vaks thought, though it was evident as she walked closer that she was certainly some sort of alien species. It was strange how much the roundness of her breasts, the curves of her hips, the coy look in her green eyes, all seemed so human. Vaks was getting aroused.

Javier's knowing eyes caught the expression on Vaks' face, and he subdued a smile.

"My honored guests," the Governor said with the manner of a royal proclamation. "I welcome you to Cantor!"

"Thank you for your hospitality," Vaks said, his voice was a dark and quiet juxtaposition to the Governor's magnanimous air.

"You must be exhausted from the journey!" he said, clapping hands on their shoulders.

Vaks felt a repulsive tremor at the touch and managed to contain his grimace only barely. His reaction was noticed because the Governor awkwardly retracted his arms and did not attempt to touch

Vaks again.

"I heard you were delayed by some ruffians at the Outskirts," he said, offering the path inside his tower to Vaks and Javier. "If you'll come with me, I'd be happy to treat you to the best of what Cantor has to offer."

"What is it that you want from me?" Vaks said, his feet planted firmly on the ground.

The Governor's broad grin dissipated into a smirk. "I need your help with a matter. A simple matter really, just one that requires a man of your credentials." His face had grown dark as he spoke, and as he lifted his head back up into the light, he grinned and said, "but you look weary and could probably use some refreshment."

"No," Vaks said, his own face harboring a burning darkness. "Tell me what you want now. Then, if we have an agreement, we can talk about refreshment."

Javier shot an indignant look at Vaks.

The Governor's smile disappeared, and he swallowed grimly. "Very well. Let's go to my study. Fintheena, please go and make sure that Barnaby is well treated. We owe a lot to him for doing this." The fox woman nodded. As she was turning, her glance shifted to Vaks, and she winked. This slight gesture sent blushes to his stern cheeks, melting his tough exterior and revealing the sensitive romantic inside.

Fintheena giggled, taking Barnaby by the elbow and leading him off. Vaks let the blood return back to the rest of his body and resumed his bitter expression.

"Right this way please," the Governor said. He looked at Vaks and smiled warmly. "I think you are going to like it here."

The way through the Governor's tower was a magical journey in itself. The passageways were filled with relics and artifacts of the ages of the past universe. It seems that the most relevant pieces of human and alien history were carried onto the Edge of Time and gathered here.

An obsidian statue of a man with devil horns and a brilliant wingspan, holding up an hourglass as though it were Atlas's world, stood prominently among the collections. It was hard to keep up with the Governor and still look at the wonders around him, but Vaks was the one who wanted to be direct about the conversation, so there was no complaining if he didn't have time now to meander through the museum.

They turned a corner and entered two wooden doors gleaming from their varnish. Inside was a room that resembled a great hall more than it did a study. The ceiling was an arched dome with towering walls lined with books. There was a rail system with two ladders that could be shifted around. The far end of the room was transparent glass, and beyond the mahogany desk and through that invisible plane was Cantor.

Vaks could see the sprawling lights of inner Cantor end at the luminous purple forcefield. Beyond was pure darkness, save the dull orange glows of firelight scattered across the Outskirts.

"Now," the Governor said, "our introductions are in order I do believe. My name is Governor Cartwright. I have been providing the gentle dominion over this great city for three hundred and thirty-six years this next month. I am the provider of shelter and sustenance for more than two thirds of surviving life forms, and I ensure that all cyborgs have the Blue Blood they need to survive."

"I don't give a damn about your resume Governor Cartwheel. You sent someone here to pick us up because you want something from me, which I assure you, I am not inclined to give. So please tell me what necessitates your intrusion on my life before I lose my mind and leave you in pieces."

"Vaks, maybe you should just let the Governor talk," Javier

said.

"No..." the Governor said, lifting a hand to stifle any further retort. "Vaks is right. There is a unique situation I think you can help in. I'm going to make a drink, however, and I'll tell you about it as I do. If wc are going to proceed this way, we might as well not hold anything back. Could I make one for you as well?"

"A man of wisdom and tact!" Javier said, grinning. "I would love a drink."

A smirk escaped Vaks' mouth for a brief instant and he said, "Fine, I'll have a drink, too."

"Excellent!"

As the Governor prepared them each the three stiff drinks that none of them would have the chance to finish, Vaks heard the story of how a rogue StoryTeller had appeared in the desert some twenty years ago and had taken residence in a nearby city. What made the situation problematic was that the StoryTeller began teaching the philosophy of the StoryTellers, denouncing the debauchery and indulgence that Cantor was known to celebrate.

Normally a situation like this would be easily resolved because people naturally gravitate toward what is raunchy and rich, but for reasons the Governor didn't understand, they were converting. People really took to the temperance that the StoryTeller was teaching, and started fleeing the city to go live in Humana where the Followers of the Lighted Story keep their quarters.

What further complicated the issue was that it was causing a steep drop in profits from several different industries that the Governor endorsed. It wasn't so much of an effect that Governor Cartwright was in danger of collapsing financially, but it was just enough to irritate him. He had tried having the man assassinated, but his acolytes were surprisingly deft and capable in combat. He simply had to resort to creative means of handling the situation.

When he heard that another StoryTeller had shown up in town, he knew that he had to get to him before the Followers of the Lighted Story did. He needed a chance to show Vaks how wonderful Cantor was. He even offered a paid residence and regular income if Vaks would choose to abandon his quest and live in the futile exultance of Cantor's writhing masses.

The entire idea was that if Vaks celebrated Cantor's merits, then the Governor could make sure that the rest of the people see that the StoryTellers can exist in Cantor, too. It might lessen the effect of people leaving Cantor for simple, meager lives.

"Frankly, Governor," Vaks said swirling his glass around, having listened disinterestedly to the Governer, "I don't give a rat's ass about the teachings of temperance and compassion, or your Story for that matter. I threw that garbage out a long time ago. In fact, I would be happy to accept your offer of residence here, but not until my job is done."

Perturbed by the impetuousness of his guest's inattention, Vaks having made no effort to conceal his favor of drink over the Governor's words, the Governor sneered. "What is the object of your mission then?"

"To murder the StoryTeller."

The Governor's face became a blank stare. It dawned on him what Vaks meant, and he burst into laughter. The mirth was contagious and Javier chuckled with him. "You mean you are going to kill the man I need taken care of?" He held up his glass for a toast. "Then I will give you every resource I have at my disposal to help you in your quest. It would be my delight to see that man and his followers strung up by their feet and crucified the good old-fashioned way!"

Vaks smiled, his eyes wolfish in the shadows of his brow.

"Here's to a beautiful new future, for the last days of time!" The Governor was inflated and proud, lifting his glass in the air. As

Vaks raised his to join him, there was a thunderclap and a rush of wind.

Glass, fire, and debris exploded into the room, and the three of them were thrown onto the floor away from the window. Dust and smoke filled the air and Vaks could hear shouting. A woman's voice barked out orders to search the library, which were relayed by the husky bark of an alien. It looked decisively male with arachnid features and two extra limbs.

Vaks' ears were ringing. He sat up and looked around. Javier shook his head clear from the blast. Vaks saw worn leather combat boots approaching him, glass crunching beneath each step. He stood up from the floor and looked at a furiously attractive cyborg girl with a terrifying metal arm. It was the petulant way she looked at Vaks that really set his violent heart beating.

Something thrust against him from behind, and in order to avoid colliding with her, he twisted his body out of the way.

Before he could steady himself, however, he heard her snap an order for her men to seize them both. In the short moment between when that order had been given, and the neural destabilizing shock administered, he realized that the Governor had gotten away. The electrons then touched the base of Vaks' skull and sent him into temporary oblivion.

Chapter 21 - Cartin and Vaks

Vaks awoke and woozily came to his senses. It took a minute for his vision to fully clear, and by that time he had already formed the necessary questions to check reality. Taking in his surroundings he had no recognition of where he was or how he got there. The last memory he had was of an explosion at the Governor's study.

There was all that broken glass, and then—that girl.

She had a severe haughtiness, and seemed to have more important matters to deal with than StoryTellers and the Governor's concern over them.

Vaks was now sitting on a metal chair, his hands shackled through an iron ring on the table. Likewise, his ankles were clamped to the legs of the chair. There was no moving or getting free. He wondered if he was going to die like this, as a prisoner in a cell. He couldn't be angry. There was justice in this. His crimes necessitated a cell.

The lock clanked, and the door screeched as the guard pushed it open. The girl came walking in and sat down in the chair across from Vaks. He was able to get a good look at her. There was a long scar along her cheek from what looked like a knife fight, but it was such a clean scar that it was actually rather fetching.

She had short black hair, which stuck out defiantly in different directions, and her black eyes were as anti-suns with their intense darkness.

"Vaks Biblent. StoryTeller, right?" she said.

Vaks nodded.

Cartin waited for a verbal answer. The silence stretched painfully. Cartin's eye twitched and Vaks quietly smiled at her, his own eyes as frozen lakes of ice.

"You know this is going to be a lot easier for you if you just answer my questions. I'll let you go afterward, if I decide you don't need to die."

"Is this the way you treat all your hostages?" Vaks growled.

She lashed out across the table and hit him with her human hand. He recoiled back, the restraints clattering as they held him in place.

Cartin appeared to have surprised herself that she had hit him.

Vaks shook the shock from his head and looked up at her hurt and angry.

"I'm sorry," she said, lowering her eyes. "I…I don't know why I did that. I think maybe you deserve an explanation. I talked to your friend Javier, and I need to know how much your stories corroborate, but I'm also not going to take any chances with you…" Her voice took a severe edge. "I need you to stop looking at me like that, and tell me why you are here!"

Vaks glowered, but complied to her request. He might be indignant concerning his restraints and improper custody, but it was a simple matter he thought. One that would be easily resolved when she realized they weren't enemies. Vaks gave her the gist of what had happened since his meeting with Javier. He left out any information about why he had come to the Edge of Time, other than to say that he came here looking for a StoryTeller.

"How about you tell me why you are seeking the StoryTeller?" Cartin said, folding her hands together on the table.

Vaks' look swallowed the warmth of the room. "To give him my regards from the others. Now how about you let me out of these restraints?"

She gave him an impatient look in reply, but walked around the table and knelt beside the chair to unfasten the bonds holding Vaks' ankles. He could smell the sweat of her skin as she came close to him. When all the restraints were removed, Vaks stood and stretched, Cartin cautiously stepping back.

She seemed fairly certain he wasn't going to attack, but looked ready to defend herself anyway. Vaks eyed the metal knuckles of her cyborg arm and knew immediately that he did not want to cross blows with the girl. He made an effort not to appear hostile, but the way he stretched his jaw and barred his teeth during his stretch was undoubtedly unnerving.

"Come on," Cartin said, opening the door. "I'll answer your questions in the next room with your friend. Then we'll figure out how to get you out of here."

"Just like that?"

Cartin shrugged. "Well, we don't really have any conflicts with you. Except for the fact that your presence is the reason that the Governor got away, but that is not enough to make you an enemy, since you were only there by mistake."

Javier was waiting for them in the next room. He was sipping on a steaming cup of coffee and laughing jovially with a soldier. When he saw Vaks walk in he smiled charmingly over at him and wrapped up his conversation with the soldier.

"Glad to see you made it through the interrogation," Javier said, grinning at Vaks. "Miss Delgado can be quite serious when it comes to getting answers."

"I can see that."

"Here is the situation," Cartin said, "you two just happened to be palavering with the Governor at the wrong time. An hour earlier and you would have missed our attack, the Governor would be killed, and the people of Cantor would be free to regulate their own addictions."

"It doesn't change the fact that he was going to help us get to Humana to find the last StoryTeller," Vaks growled.

"That is what concerns me though," Cartin said to them. "Why was he willing to help you?"

"He's got a StoryTeller problem. He thinks I can help him take care of it."

"Look, how about you just tell me what your issue with the StoryTeller is?"

"The man is responsible for the extinction of my people, and happens to be the same man that the Governor has an ideological conflict with. While I won't take care of the problem the Governor's way, I will take care of it on my own. He was going to help though."

Cartin eyed them both thoughtfully. The large insectoid man walked over and whispered something in Cartin's ear with a rapid succession of clicking sounds. She nodded, spoke a short reply to him, and he walked off.

"Seems a lot of people have problems with the StoryTellers these days, though not many voices speak out against them."

"You keep talking like there are several. Is there more than one StoryTeller here?"

"Well, I guess the only proper one is the leader, but he's gathered quite a congregation of people who need something more to believe in. They call each other StoryTellers, the lot of them do. Quite frankly, I'm sick of hearing about their propaganda. You can't go anywhere in the city anymore without getting assaulted by their messages of virtue and living rightly. It's rather disgusting really."

"You want them gone too?" Vaks asked.

"Well, strictly for personal reasons, because they annoy me to hell with their preaching, and I don't need that saccharine cosmic nonsense. I want the real, raw, gritty, dark human experience that still dwells in our souls. I need to see violence for the wicked, redemption for the oppressed, and the triumph of the just. Not the complacency of the meek."

Vaks raised his eyebrow at her and smiled darkly.

"Get that look off your face and forget you ever had the idea!" Cartin snapped, her features contorting into a vicious snarl. "I'll break every bone in your body if you even think about touching me."

"I just agree with your way of thinking is all," Vaks said, his smile revealing two incisors.

"You don't know a thing about it," Cartin growled.

"And you don't know a damn thing about me!" Vaks barked angrily. "Maybe you should think about that before you lock someone in chains and hit them because you are in a foul mood!"

Cartin swung her fist at Vaks again, but he ducked out of the way in time to avoid contact.

"Vaks! Settle down!" Javier yelled, grabbing him by the arm. Javier's grip was so firm on Vaks' upper arm that he froze. He felt like Javier could tear his arm off if he only wanted to.

Cartin was breathing hard, her face flushed. "I'm sorry," she said, looking down. "I...shouldn't have attacked you like that."

"Well why did you then!"

Cartin glanced at Vaks with rage. "Because I hate your guts, that's why!"

Vaks felt his stomach drop. Blood drained from his face, and sorrow filled his eyes. It didn't matter anyway, but Cartin's unwarranted rejection of him only encouraged the flow of depression.

"Fine, you don't have to like me. But how about you let me go if you hate me so much?"

"I said I'm sorry, alright?" Cartin snapped back. "I just...reacted. I don't normally do that. I'm under control now. We'll let you go, Vaks, but I want to help you. Regardless of my personal taste for men like you, we should not have detained you. If you have business with the StoryTeller of Humana, we'll get you there and make sure you have supplies to continue your journey if you need them."

Vaks eyed her for a long moment. She did not take her hateful gaze off him, even if she did lower the intensity of its glare. She couldn't see this, but that innocent hating glare was eroding the fragments of compassion that clung to Vaks' heart.

His world was taken from him, and even now, the universe seemed to turn on him. This woman whom he might have once loved and been loved dearly by, in a different time, now seemed to hate him on pure instinct—as she should hate a man who abandoned his wife to evil, or who couldn't keep his son or tribe alive.

She didn't understand the brink of despair and loss that threatened to engulf him, and her comment hastened the demise of his humanity. Her eyes knew that he was weak, that he was afraid, that he was cowardly, but that he was the recent survivor of a massacre, she knew not, nor would she have given him sympathy if she had. She saw a truth in him, his truth, and hated it by its very nature. He recognized her perceptions of him and they drug his mind under the surface of harmony, where he gulped water in place of air, and sank into deeper depression.

Consequently, Vaks felt a biting venom toward Cartin himself. If she hated him so instinctually, he figured she at least deserved the same treatment.

"Miss Delgado," Javier added, carefully eyeing the rapid tensing of the moment, "thank you for helping us."

She turned and smiled warmly at Javier. "It's no problem at all. We take regular trips to the outer edges of Cantor. There we have a relay station of land buggies that can get us to Humana. I have business there myself and can escort you along the way."

They were in an underground subway station that had been renovated to be a transportation link between parts of the city. Most of the subway system was unexplored and forgotten about, which is what made it an ideal place for the LTR to operate in, but not without danger.

Monsters dwelt in the darkness of the underground. Beasts, irradiated and twisted by the warped environment of their dying planet ship, hid in the un-excavated darkness. A number of lives had been taken just clearing out the passages and making them safe for the headquarters. It was not uncommon, however, that a wandering nightmare would find its way in and take a life or two.

They stood outside on the platform waiting. Vaks was stoic. Javier continued his chat with a guard, and Cartin had begun speaking to the station leader who was directing the entire operation of the Multi Peak Lighthouse. That was what they called their base station, as its surface location was an abandoned lighthouse watching over a barren sea, empty of water and life.

There was a gong and then a rushing of wind as the subway came reeling up from the tracks. The fact that they could get any piece of technology operating again was a remarkable feat, but something as complex like a network of subway cars, however, was particularly impressive.

"How long did it take you to turn the subway back on?" Javier asked.

"Only about three months once we got the team together to really work on it."

The doors hissed open and inside the cars were walls of computer equipment, and two soldiers who appeared to be eagerly awaiting guests.

"Come on," Cartin said, stepping aboard the subway. "It's going to be about two hours before we reach our stop."

"Excellent!" Javier said. "Maybe Vaks can tell us a Story!"

Vaks shot Javier a dark look.

"Oh, come on, don't be like that. I've seen the way it helps you, Vaks. You need to tell another one."

That alerted Vaks' attention and the subway door slid shut. There was a tone projected and the subway car lurched to life, causing Vaks to reach out for the handle to stabilize himself.

"What do you mean by that?"

"I mean, you had this same dark and sullen look on your face the day you trudged into my home. Once you started telling stories though, it seemed to lighten you up a bit. What do you say?"

It was in fact the very drive that Vaks needed, but Javier didn't understand the ramifications of that course of action. All these years he had thought that the rules about telling stories out in reality were nonsense, but he could now feel what they were causing to happen. There was a release in telling that filled Vaks with powerful euphoria. The effect wore off without side effects, but always with a distinctive visit from Entropy.

It only seemed to give Entropy more power over Vaks' mind. All those stories he had told Javier were the final nails in the coffin for Vaks, giving Entropy enough energy to embed all of its clawed nails into the softness of his soul.

Telling would make him feel better, but it would bring Entropy upon him with greater and greater force. It was beginning to get hard distinguishing between the real conversations happening around him and the thoughts of un-wisdom that Entropy whispered constantly in his ear, telling him to abandon his quest to melt away in Cantor in stupefied drug use. To end his life and give up the job that had somehow left him out. He should be dead with the rest of his tribe.

"Alright, I'll tell you a Story," he said, and looked at Cartin with a wolfish smile. "Let's let the guards pick the subject of this one, however."

Vaks turned to one of the men and raised an eyebrow inquisitively. "Sir, is there a Story you would like to hear about?"

The guard was quick to answer. "Actually…I have one in mind that maybe you can tell."

Vaks motioned for him to continue.

"You see, my grandmother used to tell me about the StoryTellers of long ago. She told me about how the first StoryTellers were chosen by the Paragons of Consciousness from Earth. She said that Earth was our origin planet all those ages ago. I can't seem to find any information about the planet though. Do you know what happened to Earth?"

Vaks closed his eyes and smiled. "I know of what became of that tragic planet. It is not one you may like the answer to, but I will tell you."

Chapter 22 - Earth

This is the end of the age of Earth; a Story of the greater past where StoryTellers only go during their initial training, or if they are hunting a particularly obscure topic that leads them to the very beginning.

During the maturing of Earth, the humans that populated the planet evolved their consciousness through the means of a primitive form of StoryTelling. These primitive forms took on a life of their own and became the divided nations that incited the Golden Age of Earth. They had evolved from an organism that initially survived on primal animal instincts, but gradually came to submit its life force to the will of humanity.

Their Stories, which empowered them to dominate the natural organism from which they evolved, Earth, clashed with growing global conflicts that ensued from an inability to separate their animalistic nature from their ideological Selves, who told the Stories. Ultimately, Earth itself was awakened by the distress and destruction that primitive humanity was causing to its flesh and blood and involved itself.

Earth called forth the Paragons of Consciousness, who came to inhabit the thirteen heroes who united the stories of all the human organisms, and together transformed humanity into a creature capable of developing technologies that could traverse intergalactic distances. These were the same Paragons of Consciousness who came again in the final years, during the construction of the Edge of Time.

For several millennia, Earth's divided nations were always at each other's throats for land and resources, which were in reality their ideological differences causing them to war with even more fervor than human instinct demanded to survive. At last the culmination of primitive human StoryTelling led to the final holy war where the prophesied apocalypses culminated into a cataclysm that finally ended the cycle.

Earth was not prepared for the colossus that rose from the ocean's depths. Nor for the black wind that gave un-life to the corpses of the earth, which began clawing their way from the depths of their tombs.

It seemed that the very crust of the earth opened up a portal to a realm inside the planet that habituated only the most infernal and diabolical creatures of the human imagination. When the scaled and cloven-hoofed nightmares came crawling into reality, the planet cracked.

All hope for salvation was ended and humanity was thrashed and scattered into confusion as the world fragmented into desolation.

There was a hero who arose during that time: Ruen the Unborn, who was the first consciousness to evolve beyond the limits of human nature and come to exist entirely as an independent conscious Story. He was a horror and fright to all the warring realms. Ruen was a man who possessed extraordinary skill in employing the Art of Story and was among the first to have seen the future that the Paragons of Consciousness could teach. Though he was only manipulating consciousness to a degree much lower than what future Story-Tellers are able to do, the capacity of his power was legendary nonetheless.

Stories claim that Ruen the Unborn was able to exert his will so powerfully on the forces of nature that he could call fire from the sky and water from the dry earth. His was the rallying force that fended off the impending destruction of humanity by a cosmic unbalance. Something had gone desperately wrong on Earth and the portals of the universe had been torn open by the swelling forces of extra dimensions.

The apocalypses of earth eradicated most of the population, but the survivors were a combination of infernal beasts and heavenly hosts which had turned their allegiances to Ruen the Unborn, the leader of the human race during that time. When peace was ensured, the fires of war extinguished, and the nightmares banished, then came the arrival of the Paragons of Consciousness.

The world was still in shambles, the technology of their great cities in ruins, but the strange resplendent beings, blinding in their light, gave a special gift of knowledge to the humans. They brought with them years of scientific progress in a single instant, and transmitted that knowledge across all of Earth's consciousness, giving fire to silicone life in the process.

It was a revolutionary way to think, uniting the driving forces of humanity and the planet into a single will; it enabled the rapid redevelopment of their civilization. They introduced an entire field of science that humanity had not yet discovered, and soon the problems of intergalactic travel were solved. This new science was derived from the dark energy filling the universe, which later coalesced into something known to one man as Entropy.

This time was the dawning of the Golden Age of humanity. The Age of Ignorance had passed, and humanity became aware of the presence of sentience in silicone life, which they had crafted by their own will, to cast off the binds of religion for them. It liberated them from destroying themselves, but doomed them to the will of a superior form of life who depended on them for survival as well. As humanity began the rapid construction of Gravity's Door, the first system employed for intergalactic travel, the Paragons of Consciousness took select individuals from Earth, removing them from reality.

The closest friends of Ruen were taken, Ruen himself being lost in the outcome of the apocalypse. They were his widow, his best friend, his captain, and the remaining nine who were integral in the defeat of the armies of armageddon.

What became of Earth after that is rather tragic. The apocalypse had caused irrevocable damage to the planet itself and it rapidly decayed. It seemed that so many inter-dimensional fluctuations had caused unforeseen consequences for the solar system. It was a very strange time for Earth as the dimensional effect of the Paragons of Consciousness being present in reality, mutated organic material in people's brains.

It is said that the deities and forces of collective symbolism began manifesting themselves in the corpus of humanity, causing mayhem around the world. By the time the construction of Gravity's Door was complete, the state of the Earth had gotten so bad that people could not even go outside of the shelters and into the blasted environment without special protection from symbolic rites or technology.

Why some people were more receptive to performing the Story rites and mysteries that were possible, and why some people were only able to use technology, remains a mystery; but when the device was completed, the coordinates for the first colonies chosen, and the missions prepared, humanity began dividing again. These were the last survivors of Earth's Story, and they had rallied together to survive the end of Earth's intended existence, stepping through the liquid field and appearing in their new homes across the universe.

They began with three colony missions. It was all their scarce resources could afford, but it would have to be enough. With the technology of the Gravity Door, they would easily be able to exchange the benefits of their particular world instantly across the universe.

Nearly every last living person left Earth on that day. There were a few that had stayed behind, and their sacrifice is what prevented the forces of darkness that were swallowing Earth from following the rest of humanity through Gravity's Door.

It was thus that Earth ended, the StoryTellers chosen, and humanity's conquest of the universe, begun.

Chapter 23 - Humana

"Come on," the guard scoffed. "I thought you guys were supposed to know what really happened out there!"

"You deny the truth of my tale?"

"I'm just saying that there was a lot of hocus-pocus in it, you know? I mean, all this talk about 'silicone life' and 'dark energy'? It all sounds like a bunch of crap to me."

"That is the beginning of our historical record," Vaks said. "There were no StoryTellers before then. We have to follow the recorded accounts of what people experienced and remembered from those times. It's hard to believe that there were in fact extra-dimensional monsters that appeared and attempted to destroy humanity, but that is the story as it is told.

"Despite not having any accounts of similar occurrences in the universe, the husk of Earth had significant evidence indicating the veracity of the tales," Vaks continued.

"Wait a minute!" Javier interjected. "You've been to Earth?"

Vaks shook his head negatively. "I've only read the accounts of the StoryTeller who went there. He was able to duplicate the success of the rites that were performed and could walk around the scorched husk of the planet, immune to the hostile environment's effects on his sanity." Vaks tilted his head noncommittally. "That is what the books say at least. I've never seen anyone do a rite like that, nor even heard about it. Those rites were locked anyway when a number of murders occurred in the attempt to perform them by students. Again, this is just what I've read."

"But you've never seen anything like a demon in your entire life?" the guard said shakily, delighting Vaks that the story had made him nervous.

"Now that, on the other hand, is up for speculation."

The guard looked at Vaks, puzzled. "What do you mean?"

"Evil and darkness manifest themselves supernaturally often in the course of human history, as do light and virtue. That can seem demonic to some."

"What kind of people have you seen like that!"

"That's enough Frinkle!" Cartin snapped. "You aren't here to listen to Stories. You are here to keep us safe from the Governor's assassins. So quit jabbering, and start getting your head in your job."

The man paled. "Yes, ma'am!"

Vaks laughed. "Oh, come on! You may not believe me or want to hear this, but the exercise of the imagination with a StoryTeller is one of the most beneficial experiences a human can have!"

Cartin rolled her eyes, but Vaks thought he detected a small smile in her petulant expression. It vanished quickly, but not before he noticed that there was a warm part in her heart that had not been completely embittered by the world. It was a sense he had a keenness for. He always excelled at recognizing the embers of humanity that revolved around the heart. Not that he thought she was in love with him or anything, but there was certainly a collision of chemicals that sparked that half-smile that had hardly ever even existed.

The subway lurched to a stop and the time for telling the tales of the universe had ended. Their journey had recommenced, and now they were only several hours away from the temple where the Story-Teller responsible for Vaks' wrath resided.

As they exited the station, Cartin was exceptionally adept at dealing out orders and mustering her crew for tasking. She paid little attention to Javier or Vaks, but knew exactly what needed to be done to make the preparations to take the Land Buggy across the wastes to Humana. It was a short journey, but one that could still be hazardous. She clearly didn't want to take any chances and had it loaded out for a long expedition, just in case.

Vaks was impressed by how well-respected and trusted Cartin was by her crew. At first glance, she appeared to him nothing more than a sullen young woman barely out of her teens, who had a high-tech prosthetic and no boyfriend. She was, in fact, a decisive and firm commander, whose orders were obeyed without question. She even gave a small parting speech to the lieutenant that was going to command under her absence.

His eyes even seemed to tear up as she spoke to him. Vaks snorted softly to himself.

"There's no need to mock a man's respect for a woman," Javier said sternly.

"I wasn't mocking!"

"Yes, you were."

"Well, seriously though. The man is about to cry because his commander is leaving for a bit."

"Take another look," Javier said.

Vaks looked back and watched the man's eyes as he saluted.

"That man is tearing up because he knows he is never going to see her again. He knows you have taken her from him."

As his last word fell into Vaks' ear, the lieutenant turned a dark glare towards him. Entropy ran its fingers through the back of Vaks' head, sending chills of energy through his body. He grinned violently at the man, showing his incisors.

"What are you grinning about?" Cartin asked directly at Vaks, who beamed delightfully at her.

"A brilliant idea just occurred to me."

"Well keep it in your head because we're ready to roll," Cartin said, walking past Vaks and stepping into the driver's seat of the Land Buggy. "Grab a seat and hold fast. This baby flies over the dirt!"

Cartin had not exaggerated; she propelled them at over a hundred miles an hour over the surface of the planet, leaving a blade of dust dividing the charred landscape behind them. As they escaped the looming shadow of Cantor, the earth seemed less burnt. It became grayer, with sparse patches of brown sand in some basins.

By the time they reached Humana, they were in a brown desert sparsely spattered with tufts of bristly grass. The Land Buggy rolled to a stop outside of the gates of the city. This place seemed the polar opposite of Cantor to Vaks.

There were no outskirts for that matter. The city itself probably did not exceed five miles in diameter. The outer wall was a small stone structure that did not rise more than four feet. It was made of tan stones, was crumbling throughout the mortar, and had completely collapsed in some spots. The gateway had pillars holding the fixtures for what was an enormous wooden door that now lay discarded on the side of the road.

They entered within and saw that the houses were made of an adobe mold that was crumbling away at the corners,. There were some houses made of stacked stones which appeared to be in much worse condition than the adobe. The temple and the square surrounding it, however, were constructed with fine stone cut by expert masons.

The edges of the planes were perfect geometries. The stone

was smooth and polished. Not a crack or blemish in the material could be seen, and the immensity of the temple itself radiated this immaculate structure like a beacon of defiance to all the forces of disorder.

The square was bustling with people and aliens. There were tables and tents lining the edges, throngs of people milling about between them.

Vaks could feel the presence of his target within. He could feel the culmination of his rage and vengeance being answered here in the next few minutes. All he had to do was make it up those steps into that festering temple of vile murdering wretches and evict them from existence.

"Vaks," Javier said, putting a hand on his shoulder, "are you alright?"

"Get your hand off me."

Javier retracted his hand and frowned. "You are looking a little...tense."

"Am I?" he said, his voice louder than he intended. "Why do you think that is?" Vaks was clenching his fists, his fingernails cutting into his skin.

He wondered why it was so dark outside in the middle of the day, looking around the sky for the sun. He found it and recoiled away from its brightness. It wasn't dark outside. It was the people. Their faces were darker. Not their faces, but their eyes. Each of them was fixed on him with their black watchful orbs, despite what the others were doing.

As they turned their heads away, the obsidian orbs followed Vaks still through the backs of their skull. Vaks started trembling as he felt the feeling of Entropy emerging in his mind.

Vaks was then pushed out of his own mind, and left standing helplessly at the edge of his sanity, as the Entropy running rampant in his mind took control of his faculties. Vaks had wanted to surrender. He had wanted to give in to the feeling. It wasn't a surrender of control as much as it was a partnership. They had the same goal.

His feet moved forward on their own accord. Vaks shoved people out of the way, making his way through, Cartin and Javier following him, protesting words he never spared the attention to hear.

He reached the base of the steps and attempted to pass, but was stopped by one of the acolytes.

"Sir, access to the temple is restricted to all but initiates and ordained, except during public hours. You can come back and use the library or cathedral tomorrow during the three hours on either side of the zenith."

Vaks turned his Entropic gaze to the man and felt the firmness in the man's conviction to the Story. He could sense the faith through Entropy's nose like a body odor. It delighted the animal inside, inciting him to stretch his claws.

"Your faith is false. The universe is mine now. Entropy is the pervading law."

The man dropped his sigil and stumbled back.

Vaks heard a sound from behind him but ignored it. All he wanted to hear was the sound of his heart beating in his ears. He wanted to feel every cell in his body as he exulted in the destruction of life.

His vision nearly blacked out as he reached savagely for the man's throat. His eyes bulged in fear, but he was unable to scramble away. Vaks held him fixed in place by his eyes alone.

At last...blood again at last!

It was a thought that never tasted its desire. Cartin struck him firmly across the face, her right fist colliding with his skull, sending shocking pain across it.

Entropy released Vaks' mind, and he stumbled back. He moaned and stretched his jaw painfully, wincing as he rubbed the growing bruise. "What the hell was that for?"

Cartin gave him a confused look. "'Cause you were about to kill that man, that's why! What the hell is wrong with you!" She was standing cautiously away from him, as was Javier.

The man who had been released cried out and scrambled to his feet, alerting the other acolytes.

"Vaks," Javier said cautiously, as if approaching a dangerous animal. "What has gotten into you?"

Vaks looked at the panicked man fleeing and sighed. "It's time to end this, Javier. I won't wait any longer."

There was a silence as the three of them let the awareness of what had happened sink in. Vaks had become an increasingly unstable individual, and he had nearly killed an innocent man for no reason other than to satisfy some inner beast.

"Excuse me!" a nasal voice announced from the stairs.

The three of them looked at the newcomer. It was a gaunt, priestly looking man with a shaved head and skin that seemed stretched so tight over it that it might be used as paper.

"Lord Alastair, the Paragon of the Enlightened Story, will speak with you. Your arrival has been long expected."

Vaks looked plaintively at Cartin and Javier, who offered no words, and turned back to the messenger. "Very well, lead the way."

They followed in silence, Javier and Cartin staying equally distant from Vaks. It seemed the devil himself had possessed Vaks, taking the form of his flesh and fusing with his spirit.

The temple cathedral was enormous and ornate. Lavish metal work adorned the buttresses and pillars of the supports. In the center was a massive golden sphere. Below it was a throne upon which Alastair, on a cushion, sat cross legged.

His face was serene; his posture relaxed and strong. His hair had grayed over the years on both his head and his beard. His eyes, however, were so kind and wise that it seemed impossible that he was able to order the murder of a human being.

It took Vaks off guard, who was not prepared to see someone who radiated good so completely, that even Entropy was enraged by it.

"Welcome, Vaks," Alastair said, his voice as pleasant as his demeanor and carrying a frightening amount of power within it. "We have much to discuss about Entropy."

Chapter 24 - Alastair

"What does Entropy have to do with anything?" Vaks spat back, but before a response could be given, interrupted himself "It doesn't matter. Answer me this: Why did you kill the StoryTellers?"

"Because their dim-witted, self-serving sociopathic actions brought Entropy into existence!" Alastair snarled, startling all three of them. His attendants seemed unperplexed by the outburst. "Your lusting and pursuing that lust with the Stories you told about the places you went brought this whole temple of life crashing down upon us. It's your fault!" He pointed a finger, antagonizing Vaks, stabbing his last syllables.

When he was finished, the aura of peace and serenity settled upon him as gently as a sheet upon a mattress.

"Now," he said calmly, "to answer your question so we can move on to more important matters; I killed them because the balance had been shifted. The efforts of the StoryTellers to preserve the life of the universe inadvertently hastened the destruction. Every attempt to prevent a calamity, whether it was social, political, natural, or otherwise, would only increase the speed of decay."

"But what did I have to do with it?" Vaks demanded.

"Your behavior on Jal marked the end of hope. It was too much abuse of the power that was entrusted to you. The balance was put in the favor of Entropy and from the universe, Entropy evolved itself from the collective consciousness it dwelled within—of that consciousness that exists in the fifth realm. That which is in all the realms at once, and equally in none."

"Hold on a second," Cartin interjected. "What the hell is the fifth realm?"

Alastair sighed, and Vaks turned to her.

"Think of all of consciousness as made of elements of thought the same way that atoms and molecules make up matter. Now these elements scattered about can be manipulated and shaped, stressed and mixed—any number of things, to create different results. The whole field of study where this science is possible is called the fifth realm. It's also only accessible through sentience."

"As I was saying," Alastair continued, "from that substance has come sentience independent of ours. Evolved from us is the higher state of evolution. We are nothing compared to what it is capable of. It is the culmination of the gods and goddesses of humanity, forcing its way into a skin of its own, manifesting with the will it learned from humanity, the impossible. The fundamental forces of consciousness are fighting their way into an existence of their own."

"Why did we fight so hard against it then, if this is our evolved form?"

"No, Vaks," Alastair said, shaking his head. "It is not *our* evolved form. It is its *own* life form."

Silence hushed the room as Vaks considered this. The frightening prospect suggested that the very concepts and characters of fictional Stories could rise up and become real forces in the physical universe.

Vaks knew Alastair was right. He had read on the subject, and though he had not thought of it in this way before, it only seemed to complete his understanding of the universe. It was not the characters that would rise up and take form themselves. It was the Stories that could do this. If so motivated, these Stories, thriving from the energy of the universe, could spontaneously manifest in the existence of consciousness!

It was too late to test these theories, Vaks thought as he scratched his chin considering what Alastair had told him. The universe was about to end, and no such willful manifestation of creation as this had occurred before, that Vaks knew anything about at least. It would likely never happen anyway. It made sense that it would be Entropy, however. Entropy was the major force of existence. The primal force of undoing.

"You understand now, don't you, Vaks?" Alastair said. "You woke up Entropy by upsetting the balance and creating Stories with your will. By staying on Jal and living like one of its citizens, you, whose power resides only in the strength of observing Stories, unbalanced the universe beyond correction."

"Shut up…" Vaks muttered.

"NO!" Alastair shouted, standing up. He was towering over them on his throne. He wore white robes and his voice was the booming resonance of the almighty. "You used your power to create a Story that had no business being created, and now you are suffering the consequences!"

"SHUT UP!"

"NO, VAKS!" Alastair screamed, leaping off his throne and grabbing the chest of Vaks' robes. "If the StoryTellers would have not tried to fight the growing corruption, their demise would not have been necessary." He released Vaks, shoving him away. "As it is, without my interference, they would have hastened the destruction to so great an extent as to prevent Javier's people from forging the Edge of Time."

Cartin shot Javier a surprised look when she heard this.

"They had to die."

From the realization of his own contribution to the utter destruction of everything, Vaks had grown pale and empty. He knew it was true. He knew it because it was the kind of thing Entropy would whisper in his ears. He knew he was destroying everything, but he didn't know to what extent. For Vaks to have not told stories would have crippled him psychologically. It was in his very nature to do so, and many people needed to hear them for their own sanity, on the planets he visited.

There was no way he ever imagined that the repercussions of his actions would be as catastrophic as the demise of the universe, but he was aware of the strange dark voice that urged him on as he continued his life on Jal.

Everything that he loved was gone now. His people had been killed by the man standing before him for no better reason than because *he* thought it was better to exterminate them.

"You could have stopped them. You could have told them that they were inadvertently destroying the universe. You didn't have to murder them," Cartin said.

"What do you know about it? Have you ever lived with the threat of Entropy?" Alastair snapped.

"What do you know about human life if you're so quick to kill?" Cartin spat back.

"I HAVE LIVED LIFETIMES YOU'VE NEVER IMAGINED COULD EXIST!" Alastair bellowed. "What do you know of life? You..." he scoffed, pointing at Cartin with distaste, "you...urchin clinging to the fringes of existence! You know about as much of life as the mold clinging on the edge of the toilet basin does."

Cartin's rage began opening into a tirade that would lambast Alastair, but she was stopped by Vaks before she could begin.

"Alastair..." Vaks' voice was a steady flow of controlled fury. "Tell me what you want. If this has to do with Entropy, then tell me what it is."

Alastair met Vaks' gaze with an equal darkness that did not seem entirely human. It was a darkness that seemed substantial and vibrant, as if it might crawl out of his eyes like a shadowy parasite that swallows life into its expanding gullet.

"You see it, don't you?" Alastair said, not taking his eyes off Vaks.

Vaks knew he was looking at Entropy in the eyes of Alastair. He knew that it was the very same darkness that had been his companion, that was also Alastair's.

"I'll ask you one question, Vaks," Alastair said. "This will decide who will continue."

Vaks kept his gaze tightly on Alastair, ready to leap into action at any moment. He knew better than anyone present what kind of damage the StoryTellers were capable of, especially when they were in snowy old age. He felt the mental probe reach his thoughts and repulsed it from him, spitting venomously. "You'll get nothing from me, Alastair!" Their eyes locked across a beam of rage. "Death needs neither questions nor answers."

Alastair paled. "She gave me those same words."

"Who?"

Alastair was gritting his teeth in uncontrollable rage. "She gave me that same look, too!"

Vaks saw then, in the countenance of Alastair, something so familiar and frightening that he couldn't spare another moment of inaction.

"There is an easier way than this," Alastair growled. "You can submit your will, and I will carry Entropy with me, for all of us, to the Halls of Remembrance."

Vaks was losing patience. He felt the threads of the Great Story weaving around him, the awestruck acolytes engaged in frozen observance to see such a clash. StoryTellers were legendary on the Edge of Time, and their powers should cooperate, not oppose.

I can't exist in more than one, Entropy said, whispering in Vaks' ear, a phantom shadow lurking among them all. *This is why I have brought you here.*

Alastair knew the moment Vaks did and struck out, crashing his fist into Vaks' jaw. Vaks stumbled backwards and fell to a knee, but quickly sprang upward with his coiled legs and crashed his fist into Alastair's chest. He went flailing backwards, tumbling over his throne, and the brouhaha commenced.

It was melee. Acolytes rushed in to grab Vaks, but were halted by the metallic fist of Cartin's unrelenting rage. Her strikes were fast and deadly, shattering bone into fragments that tore out of their skin as the force of her attacks impacted. A madness settled into all present, and blood and death demanded payment.

Javier ducked out of the way of a swinging pole arm, and lunged toward the attacker, pushing him off balance. He pulled his pocket knife out and leapt onto the attacker, screaming wildly. His eyes flared with desperation, terrifying in their resolve to kill.

The knife plunged into the acolyte's chest. Blood spurted and the young man gasped in pain and terror. The blade went down again, and again, piercing at last with finality. Javier looked up from his kill like a wild animal, drinking in the chaos of fighting that so quickly had begun.

Alastair was on his feet, preparing to defend the coming attack. Vaks was midair, leaping from the throne he bounded across, his knee leading his momentum. Alastair tried to lift his hand up to protect his face, but he was not fast enough. Vaks' knee collided with Alastair's head, sending it, and the rest of his attached body, soaring backward in a graceful arc.

Vaks was in pursuit. He knew the minute Alastair's fist impacted with his chin that the man was going to die. Vaks knew much about martial arts, despite his inexperience with violent situations. He knew by the force and speed of the blow that his own skills far exceeded Alastair's. It was, in fact, his favorite topic of instruction.

Vaks placed his knees on the shoulders of Alastair, pinning him, and then clutched his throat. Alastair's eyes and veins bulged with the applied pressure of Vaks' grip.

"This has nothing to do with Entropy," Vaks growled.

Alastair's eyes bulged with panic as Vaks' grip tightened. He attempted to roll on to his shoulder, kicking Vaks off him, but Vaks' fingers were deft. He knew the locations of the nerves. His fingers had trained needless hours to know instinctually where the vital life meridians connected. He clutched into the nerves like a vice. Alastair shuddered violently as Vaks pushed his head into the ground, preventing himself from being thrown off.

Alastair's eyes began to fill with blood. His lips were pressed together grossly like a fish. His skin was purple from suffocation. Underneath his flesh, the stem of his vertebrae dislodged itself in Vaks' hands, and life was severed between his body and mind. With a single resisting twitch, the spirit left Alastair's body. Vaks breathed heavily, sweat dripping from his face onto Alastair's forehead. His heart was thumping and his mind darkened out everything but the memory of Alastair's feeble pulse as it ceased.

The temple was silent about them. There were six corpses around them and surely more would join them if they stayed. Already the silence was filled with the muffled sounds of movement within the corridors.

"Come on…" Cartin said, pulling Vaks up from Alastair's corpse, her own hand grimy with gore. "We've got to go Vaks; this place is going to turn into a hornets' nest real quick." The door burst open on the far side of the temple and three acolytes came running out.

They took a single look at Alastair's body and seemed to understand, the center man holding his arms before the other two. His eyes bore the visage of injustice and despair. His leader was dead, now an image of mortality and despair whose promises of an enduring universe were gone. His eyes teared and he turned a wrathful gaze to Vaks, whose own pitiless eyes met him ounce for ounce.

The acolyte spat at Vaks' feet and turned his head away, directing the others in carrying off Alastair's corpse.

A hole opened up in Vaks as he saw this. The wisdom of those acolytes, whose tolerance of murder made his quest for vengeance drip with guilt. It was a bitter sensation and Vaks did not accept it. Alastair had to die. He wadded up a ball of spit and considered aiming it at Alastair's corpse as they gathered him up, but spat it on the throne instead.

"Let's get out of here," Cartin said furiously.

"Wait," Vaks growled. He pointed at the man taking control of the situation, warding off the recently deceased with attendants and turning away any further calls for blood. "What did he mean, 'she'? Who do you have here?"

The acolyte downcast his eyes. "Just go! Leave us be. You've caused enough havoc where there is little enough hope to hold on to. All three of you. I curse and condemn you for your blasphemy in this holy place! Leave at once."

Javier nodded gravely, his skin pale in a complexion that resembled panic, yet did not betray his own sense of presence. "This is where the road ends, Vaks; let's go while we still have a chance."

"I know, but there was something about the way he looked at me that reminded me of someone close." Vaks said, warily turning around and beginning his exit from the temple with Cartin and Javier at his side.

They began walking out of the temple, ignoring the bustling acolytes that tended to the corpses.

"Why don't they attack us?" Cartin said, glancing nervously back.

"It's that part of the StoryTeller ethos that teaches non-violence in response to violence. Alastair was probably teaching it to them," Vaks replied.

"Wait..." Vaks said, halting.

"What is it?" Javier responded.

"Did you hear that?"

"Hear what?" Cartin said.

Javier shook his head.

"Listen..." Vaks stretched his ear out with a cupped hand, directing it toward a corridor on the left. They strained to hear what Vaks was listening for, but before they could hear it Vaks' eyes widened with awareness, and he bolted.

Through the corridor, Javier and Cartin scrambling behind him, Vaks searched for the source of the sound. They could all hear it now. A woman was crying for help.

Turning down a corridor, they shoved past an acolyte who was struggling to tie his robe as he hastened from the sleeping quarters down the hall with his companion, who was also fixing his robe, close behind him. They had missed the action, or rather, were in action elsewhere when the calamity had started. Ignoring both, Vaks attempted to burst through the door opposite, but found it locked. He thudded against it with his shoulder.

"Hello?" the woman called out. "Hello!"

"Miranda!"

There was a stunned silence filled with heart beats.

"...Vaks?"

"Miranda! It's really you!" Vaks announced, leaning his ear against the door and pressing his palm affectionately against it. There was a heavy silence that followed.

"...I thought everyone was dead." Miranda's voice seemed to drain the energy from the room.

"I know..."

"But you...got away?"

"I was on a Story. I found them dead."

"I was...at the wall all day when it happened. I didn't even see it."

"I'm going to get you out of here, Miranda," Vaks said, stepping back and shifting his garments around his waist. He steadied his feet and took a breath. Vaks collided his foot with the wooden door. The door squealed as bolts were ripped from their seating. Splinters scattered as the door shifted inward, still locked, but ready to give. Vaks kicked again, grunting as he did so, moving the door another inch open. Once more Vaks kicked, roaring as he did so, and the door crashed open, the lock and latch remaining in the open frame.

Wearing the same dark robes as Vaks, her hair brown and eyes fixed with tears of joy on her savior, Miranda ran into his arms.

He caught her and held her weeping self. He wept with her, tears dropping from his eyes from a place he did not know was still alive.

"They're all dead..."

"I know," Vaks replied.

"Look," Javier said, "this is very touching and all, but quite frankly, I don't trust the fact that these folks are going to stay non-violent. I mean, you are talking about a different species that are involved, and about a people that have been living in the savage wastes of existence for a long time. Things get violent quickly here."

"You're right," Vaks said, separating himself from Miranda. "Let's get out of here."

Nicholas Bylotas

Chapter 25 - Miranda

Javier's agitation proved wise. As soon as they had made up their minds to leave the temple, the acolytes became avengers themselves. They shouted curses, throwing open doors in search of the proper target for their fury, that of which was already halfway through the city streets because of a secret exit that Miranda knew about.

Vaks continuously stole glances at her, futilely attempting to unravel the mystery of her presence. Why Alastair had kept her locked up was beyond his understanding, for she did not look hurt physically or psychologically from the captivity, but she did seem troubled in a certain way.

Vaks didn't have the time or energy to think about it at the moment as he and the others made their way through the city as furtively as they could before the alarm from the killings caught up with them. They made it outside the city walls before the alarm reached them and were quick getting into the Land Buggy.

Their escape was both fortuitous in its outcome, and an expertly executed skill set of survival and evasion, that was trained into both StoryTellers present. Vaks and Miranda were adept at remaining unseen. Cartin, on the other hand, was versed in the alleys and streets of Humana and led them through the most discreet paths.

The Land Buggy thrummed from the dirt of the wastes and the group looked back to see if anyone was following them. Their anxiety was allayed when they saw they were alone. When the excitement settled down and the city of Humana was fading into the distance, Cartin ventured the comment: "If nobody has any other ideas, the best thing for us is to go back to the subways of Cantor and regroup at headquarters. We'll at least be safe there."

"No," Miranda said, drawing all their surprised looks. "The Halls of Remembrance are real…they are here."

"What do you mean 'here'?" Vaks said.

"Off the coast of the Boiling Sea. It was how he was able to send the killer in."

Vaks brightened at her comment and asked, "So you think we should go there?"

"We have to!" Miranda said, grabbing the top of his hand. "It's our purpose! We have to go!"

Vaks looked at her with concern. "How are you feeling right now, Miranda?"

"Just fine," she said, confused. "I'm awfully glad that you rescued me though. I mean, I thought I was going to be a goner over there in that room. He kept wanting me to be his woman! Do you believe that? That man was crazy. He honestly believed he could rewrite the story of humanity!" she scoffed. "What a nut!"

"Rewrite humanity?" Vaks questioned as gently as he could, his nerves keeping him on a razor's edge.

"Yeah, like his will was actually what was going to make the universe. I mean in a literal sense too."

"Really?"

"Vaks…it's insane. It's absolutely crazy and impossible. It's the lies of Entropy that swallowed him. That is what Entropy wants…the undoing. He claimed though, that with the proper person controlling Entropy, it can be used to *create,* and hold together the resources of reality."

"What if Entropy isn't as evil as everyone thinks?" Vaks suggested. He could feel the ire blazing from Miranda's eyes.

"Don't tell me you believe him too!" Miranda snapped, to which Vaks gave her a cold look.

"Vaks..." Miranda gasped.

Vaks turned his gaze away and looked out the window.

"Oh god, Vaks, you can't let this happen! You can't let Entropy take control! There is still time left!"

"Miranda," Vaks said calmly, "I want nothing to do with the old ways you are clinging to. This is a new age, and the universe is speeding to its doom. Entropy's will is irrelevant."

"Shut up back there for a second so we can decide on which place to go!" Javier barked back at Miranda and Vaks who were sulking in their respective corners of the vehicle.

Vaks was aware of Cartin's piercing eyes taking in the entire interaction, scrutinizing his every movement with the lightning speed of instinct and naturally developed sensibilities.

"Alright," Javier said grumpily, "there is an old hotel along the road leading to the Actinid sector. The sector's destroyed, but I don't know about the hotel. It could be destroyed by mutants and Nessa killed, but we won't know until we get there. It's the best place I think we should go. If Nessa is around, she'll treat us well. I suspect she will be too. Necrodians have extraordinary life spans and are presumed to not die naturally."

Vaks raised an eyebrow, but took Javier seriously. He had heard plenty of crazy stories from people living all over the universe with extraordinary abilities, but Vaks had known better than anyone how *real* the words can be in a Story, but also how *personally real* a

Story can be. That there was a being that did not die, however. A Necrodian was an extraordinary discovery of existence. He wondered what kind of technological advances could be discovered by examining their Stories...if humanity had any time left in the hourglass that is.

"Fine," Cartin said, whipping the vehicle around. "Coordinates are inserted. Approximate time of arrival: one hundred and nineteen minutes. Make that eighty minutes." Cartin grinned, and the Land Buggy raced across the scorched ground.

"What did he want from you?" Vaks said over the rushing wind outside.

"Aside from being his concubine? To kill you."

Vaks became tense, immediately aware of the danger.

"I refused, of course," Miranda said, continuing as if nothing had happened. "I knew you would not have killed everyone. It was a ridiculously bold lie to try and convince me that *you* would have done this."

Cartin smirked, but blushed and looked away when Vaks saw her in the mirror.

Miranda glared at him. "Where have you been all these years?"

Vaks was silent, not wanting to tell her the truth. Ashamed and embarrassed for his abandonment of his vows to stay on Jal and love his woman, and even more so for allowing those feelings to exist in the first place. He burned all of them in a fiery rage that existed in the darkness of Entropy's eyes.

"Fine. You don't have to tell me."

"Miranda, I don't think you'd understand."

Miranda's anger burst through the dam, and she slapped Vaks firmly across the cheek. He took the hit with stern patience. Her hand hitting hard against his firm jaw, he never dropped eye contact with her.

"If you think I am going to pity you, you are sadly mistaken."

She held his glare, a tear welling in her eye, collecting on her eyelash like a diamond in the waning sunset. The evening star, hanging in the balance of their tension, dropping then to the seat, its gleaming brilliance dissolving into everything.

Silent tension held them fixed, while lifetimes of memories and emotions swirled uncontrollably about Vaks and Miranda. Cartin and Javier watched, Cartin from the rear view mirror, Javier through a side mirror reflecting Miranda's face.

"Miranda," Vaks said. "Entropy is not the enemy. Entropy *is* a personification that actually exists though, and that is what I am trying to tell you. Entropy is real. Entropy is here. Right now. In this Land Buggy."

Silence forced their mouths shut. Only Vaks was willing to continue. "Don't misunderstand me...I mean in a psychological sense." He said the words, but he knew they were lies. For Vaks was quite aware of the shrouded mass of darkness leering from the crevice under the seats.

"Vaks..." Miranda said softly, as if the words were a dread she did not want to face. "That is why he wanted to kill you...so he could *be* Entropy."

Vaks turned his gaze upon the depths of her eyes once more and saw the angry fire and darkness that had been Alastair's aim and goal. His nefarious plot was to summon Entropy unto him, and now his mission had failed, just like all the teachings warned such goals would result. There was, however, still a survivor whose body would contain Entropy's madness. That person was Vaks, for Miranda had not cultivated the darkness to the same extent as he had.

"Miranda, get that crazy look out of your eye," Vaks said sternly. "I'm Vaks. I am a man: a *human*. Entropy on the other hand lives in all of us. You'll find its voice too if you search for it. Though

I wouldn't bother if I were you. You'd only know pain if you started that path now."

"What the heck has gotten into you, Vaks?" Javier questioned over his shoulder to the back seat.

"What do you mean?"

"I mean, what are you talking about…this Entropy personification?"

"I am telling my friend, whom I thought was long dead, what I have learned in these most important moments of awareness. If you're not following our conversation, quite frankly I don't give a damn! Miranda is hearing what I need to tell her."

"Sure, but Vaks…"

"No, he's right," Miranda said. "I understand what he's telling me. Vaks, I'm sorry."

Vaks said nothing but turned away and looked out the window with his arms crossed, glaring at the colorful lines of scorched earth and red sunset.

They drove on in stiff silence to the hotel. Vaks fell asleep, though none of the others did. It was only a short nap, but one much needed. The Land Buggy pulled to a stop just as the starless sky engulfed them in darkness. There was a moon, which was always full at the Edge of Time, and it lit the darkness well enough to see.

They got out of the vehicle stiffly, the exhaustion of the last few days weighing upon them. Ahead stood the Necrodian Hotel. It was a pillared behemoth of broken windows and rotting lumber. A sheet, attempting to escape through the broken window, was held fast by a rusty nail that had pierced it, its tattered edges flapping in the wind. Javier stepped onto the patio. Boards creaked under his feet as he walked, and when he knocked the knocker, thunder clapped in the distance, diverting their attention with a combination of bemused and astonished expressions.

The door opened slowly, the darkness retreating from the beam of moonlight. A withered pair of gray feet stood on a dusty red rug. Their legs rose up like milky stilts into a white dress, soiled heavily with an inky black substance. Above her shrunken frame was a head that seemed more like a maw of corpse teeth than a face.

She didn't seem capable of words, but she did hiss out a blast of hot steam as she threw her arms around Javier.

When Javier relaxed and the Necrodian released him from the embrace, Javier turned to them and said, his face beaming with mirth, "Cartin, Vaks, Miranda…this is Nessa."

Chapter 26 - Nessa the Necrodian

Being in the presence of a Necrodian is a very peculiar experience. When one first sets eyes upon the life form, the initial reaction is to be so repulsed with horror that it is hard to imagine anything more frightening in the universe. Their existence is shrouded in myth more than reality, and since they are such a rare sight, the stories never describe their first meetings aptly. That is because they draw their consciousness directly from the other realm of energy that pervades existence with us. An aberration of living flesh, they breathe the dark energy of the cosmos and seem to live more in the invisible realm, their bodies a reflection of their proportion that dwells in death's kingdom.

Their bodies are thus long decomposed, their existence no longer requiring physical form. They were never able to fully detach themselves from form, however, and when Vaks met Nessa, he knew immediately upon seeing her that Necrodians are the most advanced of all carbon lifeforms. Their unknowable old age had caused the state of their bodies to become withered and decayed. The eyes being the most unsettling aspect of a Necrodian without a doubt, appearing as living black holes of consciousness upon the universe. Looking into them drained one's energy, while somehow compelling them to look closer.

It was terrifying in all regards coming across a Necrodian, and worse yet were the stories that abounded about them. Necrodians, since they were such a rarity in most parts of the Edge of Time, were often thought of as boogeymen or angels, depending on the encounters. The odd aspect of their tales was the fact that despite the infinite wisdom they seemed to contain, every story was sexually oriented.

It was in fact the Necrodian's legend to be the "most desired" sexual partner in the universe.

"Nice to meet you," Vaks said terribly awkwardly.

Nessa opened her decomposing maw slightly and ushered a gentle, seductive hiss, extending her hand out to him. Vaks could hardly take his eyes from hers, and the thought of reaching out and touching her decaying hand seemed repulsive in every way. His resolve overcame his initial disgust, and he reached out and touched her kindly.

The moment he had contact with her, his mind released his entire life's memory, both conscious and unconscious, in a single seismic surge that passed through his fingertips.

Nessa's eyes widened, the darkness reflecting the overhead lamp like stars.

Vaks immediately became entranced. He felt warmth and energy surge through his body, confidence and strength, courage and power! He felt himself filled with the fortitude to swallow the world, and then the discipline to transfer its energy into art. His was the Way of the Story. He knew it now as the vital root to all systems.

She released his hand and Vaks felt such a loss of connection that he longed painfully to be with her again. To touch Nessa and feel the magic of that touch. It made him furious that he should be taken from her, but quickly came to his senses and shook his head clear. The appearance of Nessa seemed less imposing now. Her deathly maw certainly seemed less threatening, and he wondered what it would be like to kiss such a creature.

"Nessa, my friends and I are sort of at a loose end, and I was hoping we could stay the night here and figure out where we're headed tomorrow morning. I know it's been a long time since we talked, but I would love a chance to catch up with you."

Nessa grinned widely and threw open the door, spreading her arms out in welcome. She pointed her finger piercingly at Javier.

Javier nodded his head and stepped toward her outstretched digit, closing his eyes and pressing his forehead against it. As soon as he made contact she retracted her hand with lighting speed and faced Vaks.

"Nessa is happy to host us tonight. She hasn't had any guests in many years, but she'd love for one more hurrah at the end of the universe. After all, according to Nessa, we've got…" Javier paused, "…a lot less time than everyone thinks."

"How much closer?" Cartin asked.

"So close that I'm not going to tell you because it doesn't matter anyway."

Cartin smirked with a dark delight and nodded.

"She says we are more than welcome to choose any of the rooms to stay in, though she hasn't attended to them in years, and an infestation of arachna-rats might have taken residence in one of them. Nevertheless, the dining room is probably going to be our best bet. It'll be safe here tonight." He glanced at Nessa who hissed encouragingly at him. "And she's going to provide us lots of whiskey too."

"Sounds great!" Vaks said enthusiastically, surprising Cartin with his immediate change in disposition.

Nessa held out her hand again, pointing now to Vaks forehead.

Vaks looked at the bony, blackened appendage, leaning closer to do so. She shot her hand out and touched Vaks gently on the forehead before retracting her arm.

Vaks heard a woman's voice.

"Thank you for your Story, Vaks Biblent. Yours is a place that I honor tremendously. You do not know, nor will you ever know, what your existence means to my people. Though there will come a day that you can look back on these memories and see them from a different self, in a different universe, and that day will be your awakening."

Vaks was stunned by the voice and the words. His mind flattened into silence as the words worked their way into his mind like burrowing snakes of unknowable knowledge. It was maddening to hear, but Vaks was well on his way to insanity and could only grin psychotically—to the Necrodian's delight.

Nessa didn't offer her hand to Cartin or Miranda, and instead ignored them completely, turning around and leading them toward the dining room. The hotel was lavishly decorated, but the elegance had long been buried under decades of disuse. The dining room, however, was slightly cleaner, as if the Necrodian had frequently dwelt there.

She welcomed the travelers to sit with a sweeping gesture, tossing her white dress with her movement.

"Thank you kindly," Vaks said to Nessa, smiling warmly. He set his bag down and then took a seat on the plush chair.

"You guys make yourselves comfortable, I'm going to go back with Nessa to make arrangements for payment. I am sure we can come to a…reciprocation," Javier said seductively.

Nessa smiled and tilted her head at him, extending her elbow for him to hold. Javier took the proffered arm tenderly and followed her behind the bar and into a side room.

Miranda appeared nauseous at seeing Javier's lusty eyes.

Cartin rolled her own eyes and sighed as she plopped into a chair and pulled out a pouch of tobacco. She rolled a cigarette and after she had licked it moist and sealed the paper tight, Vaks asked her if she minded if he rolled one.

She shrugged and handed the tobacco to him. Vaks slowly rolled the cigarette, closing his eyes as he licked it. Cartin watched his lips. Miranda watched Cartin's eyes.

He held the cigarette between his finger and thumb appraisingly. Satisfied with the consistent cylindrical shape, he tucked it behind his ear and lifted his eyes to make contact with Cartin.

"Whiskey for everyone!" Javier exclaimed, setting a decanter disruptively on the table. In the crook of his arm were four glasses, which he began to fill. "It's about time we drink!"

He passed the glasses around, dismissing the feeble attempts to refuse made by Miranda, who was not as enthusiastic about alcohol as Javier or Vaks.

Miranda, however, eventually accepted the whiskey after Javier's hearty encouragement, surrendering to the delight of her sins.

"To Nessa, our beautiful Necrodian host," Javier toasted. "Thank you for your hospitality and wisdom. If there was one person's company I would like to spend the final moments of time with, it's you."

"To Nessa!" Vaks said, Miranda and Cartin echoing him.

They took a drink, Javier closing his eyes in ecstasy. "To this fine stock of whiskey—the finest in the universe, known only to the Necrodians!"

"Hail!" Vaks cheered with a mirthful grin.

They drank.

"And to the StoryTellers. A dying breed. The last of the truth."

Shadows darkened the edges of the room, and Vaks looked gravely at Miranda. Within their gazes was an ineffable sorrow resultant from the loss of the Halls of Remembrance, and their entire living history with it.

They drank.

There was a heavy silence as Javier refilled the empty glasses.

"Do you think there will be anything left at the Halls of Remembrance if we go there?" Miranda asked Vaks. Accepting her new glass.

"It would be worth a look…" Vaks said.

"Hey," Javier said, sitting down next to Nessa with his glass in hand. "It doesn't even matter, there is no way to get there! Do you think The Boiling Sea is just a name?" He raised his eyebrow. "Ever since the A.I. turned and sabotaged the planet stabilizing systems, the eastern sea became a boiling, festering liquid mass of acid, contained only by the volatile storms of a shattered sky. No one has sailed it since. I think even most of the ships have been consumed by it."

"That's not true!" Miranda said. "Alastair got his minion there somehow. I don't know how he did it. He talked about going over it. He said something about a…ghost. I know it sounds crazy, but that's what he told me. He was always cryptic and confusing though. Anyway, he said that the spirit of the machine remained as a ghost. I didn't really understand what he meant."

"That's impossible," Javier grunted. "There can't be any A.I. remaining, or any ghosts of any machines. I deactivated them and the entire core of intelligence with NetMind years ago. If what he's saying is true, and there is still an A.I. left existing, it could make matters much worse."

"What even makes you think he was talking about an A.I.?" Cartin responded acidly. "Could be anything for all we know. Did he say where he was able to cross?"

"Something about Port Earth," Miranda said.

Javier and Cartin looked at each other, holding the gaze. Vaks shifted his eyes to theirs, trying to discern what those words meant to Javier. They seemed to chill his Blue Blood.

"What does that mean?" Vaks asked.

"Port Earth was one of the most...disturbing losses during the A.I. revolt. The port was located in a mountain, and was a hub that delivered supplies to the aquatic sentience. When the A.I. turned, all the entrances and exits were sealed. When investigations commenced, they found the upper half of a human body crawling out of the open mouth of the mountain, its entrails fused with a mass of wires. They killed it. When they did, the mouth of the mountain closed, and no one's been able to open it."

"That's the short version," Cartin said.

"So do you think that's where Shammal was able to cross the ocean?" Vaks asked.

Javier was uncomfortable with the idea, shuddering at the thought of taking a journey to Port Earth to open that door. "What they saw was real, Vaks. I want you to understand that. They had footage of it. Children have nightmares thinking about what's inside Port Earth. *I* have nightmares thinking about what's inside Port Earth."

"But, it'd be worth a shot to go there," Cartin said.

"I agree," Miranda replied.

"You don't understand!" Javier protested.

"Javier, what else do we have to lose?" Vaks asked. "I understand if you don't want to go, but I intend to, or die along the way."

Cartin watched him intently, holding her eyes steady as he turned his own to her.

"I'm going," Cartin said.

"What! Why?" Javier exclaimed.

"Because I want to. That's why."

"It's suicide!"

Cartin rolled her eyes and looked at Vaks. "Vaks, I'll take you and Miranda there just to see for myself."

Javier sighed and crossed his arms, sinking into the couch. "Well have fun. You can go without me."

Vaks nodded and sipped his whiskey.

Nessa, whose presence was easily forgotten, leaned close to Javier's ear and sent an explorative forked tongue across his lobe. His surliness melted into a giggle, and he smiled. "Forget it! Let's drink tonight!"

They did drink, and before long, the four of them had forgotten that they had taken lives earlier, nor were they even bothered by it. Not when the whiskey started affecting them that is. Vaks was still troubled though. Not because he had killed Alastair, however. For that, he had no remorse.

Vaks was troubled in the fundamental core of his being, troubled by the voice of Entropy, which he welcomed more and more.

As they drank two more glasses of whiskey, Miranda had shifted seats to be close to Vaks, her thigh rubbing up against his. She threw her arms around him and hugged him fiercely.

"I've missed you so much, Vaks!"

He smiled and held her.

"I think about you a lot, you know? At least I did. About your memory that is."

"What do you mean?"

"I mean when you and I…in meditation…"

"Oh!" Vaks exclaimed, blushing. "That."

Miranda giggled.

"Oh, do tell!" Javier exclaimed with perverse interest.

"Ugh!" Cartin snorted.

"Oh, we were just kids, not even seventeen," Miranda said with a nonchalant laugh.

"And?" Javier said, showing more interest than appropriate.

"Well, we sort of snuck out of mediation class and...got a bit naughty in the outer robe storage room."

"Oh no..." Vaks said, putting his hand on his face.

"It's really just a curtain at the edge of the room. I let out a little moan and the Elder heard us. He pulled Vaks out by the hair and beat him in front of everybody!" She broke into mirthful laughter in which Javier participated. "That didn't keep us apart for very long afterward though!" She nudged Vaks encouragingly, but he was not amused.

Cartin stood up abruptly, picking up the pouch of tobacco , and carried her whiskey out to the porch.

"Cartin!" Vaks called, pulling himself away from Miranda. Cartin ignored him, the door opening and closing as Vaks disengaged from Miranda, who attempted to hold him there.

She lashed out a vice-like grip, clutching in her constricting fingers Vaks' wrist. He halted and brought a chilly, level gaze down upon her. Miranda coldly let go of his arm and shrank back in her seat.

Shaking from the energy and rage leftover from Miranda attempting to hold him in place by the arm, Vaks grabbed his whiskey and went outside, joining Cartin without a word.

The moon hung over the horizon colossally.

There was a pale green tint to its smooth spherical surface. No craters on this moon, as Vaks had come to expect on every moon he gazed upon. It was perfect in every way it seemed. Full, bright, and compelling.

Vaks and Cartin leaned over the porch rail for several minutes in silence gazing at it. The muffled laughter of Miranda and Javier could be heard through the fissures of the decrepit hotel. The scorched rock they had crossed gleamed like an oil slick, and Vaks forgot in that moment everything that had troubled him.

He was aware of Cartin. Of how close her fingers were to his on the rail. He could smell her through the night, not a perfume or artificial scent, but the fragrance of natural humanity. He liked the smell of her sweat.

"So this is it, isn't it," Cartin said as though talking to herself.

"The end of all things," Vaks muttered in agreement.

"Do you think it was for anything?"

"What was?"

She gave him a bored look that cracked his sullen temperament.

Smiling warmly, he said, "Cartin, whether or not I have any knowledge of that answer is irrelevant. Because we're not going to stop, are we? Even if there was a point and we found out it was already accomplished. Even if the point was for us to die, we'd still keep on fighting, wouldn't we?"

She didn't answer him. The question hung charged in the air.

Vaks didn't know how he knew who Cartin was, nor would he have been able to utter her true name, but he knew her nonetheless. He had known her for ages it seemed.

Her fingers sent electricity up Vaks' arm as she pulled him toward her, staring into his dark eyes. Together the two held the moonlight in the spheres between them.

His jaw tensed.

Her brow narrowed.

Metal fingers slid across Vaks' face.

His own hands were on her cheeks.

They kissed recklessly and with violent passion. Tears ran down Cartin's face, quenching the fires of his darkness with the thirst of their lips. The energy passing between each other acted as a catalyst for their awakening.

He could hear Entropy laughing and clapping behind him as they separated. There would be no happy ending for them, this seemed to threaten. This Vaks understood as sure as he knew himself. Theirs had been, and always would be, a tale that shifted between happiness and woe, with love binding them inevitably together.

How could he tell her right then that he loved her more than anything in the universe? That their lives, many times over in the scope of time, had brought them here at last against the will of the universe. For only outside the universe, on The Edge of Time, would that strange compelling force, the one that imploded upon itself during the awakening of Entropy, be unable to separate Vaks and Cartin.

These were strange Stories that Vaks had within his mind. They were the mythos of the cosmos. They were heroes of light and dark who stood and fell at the moments when time changed. Now it seemed that those symbols and heroes from the legends before the StoryTellers were real. They were the voices that guided him, the movers of the world. They were the ones that revealed the truth between he and Cartin.

How could he show her this knowledge? How could he tell her about this love? How could he convey the ancient heroes of the first stories on earth to her? Their symbols drove on through the universe, regardless of time and space. They were everywhere, Vaks saw. They lived in the lives of great people throughout time. With new names and new bodies, these archetypes of Story returned into the people whose lives caused the events that StoryTellers recorded.

Vaks looked into Cartin's eyes, loving deeper than he conceived possible, and saw through the reflected darkness that she too had a revelation of her own.

Chapter 27 - Necrodian Tears

Tears welled in Cartin's eyes. She slapped Vaks across the face, stinging his cheek. He didn't react. He took the strike as seamlessly as if they had rehearsed it.

She slapped him again.

He caught her arm.

"Cartin..."

"Don't, Vaks."

They looked at each other, fury and rage boiling in Cartin's eyes. She contained the very essence of fury, drawing Vaks in, the remaining vestige of light within him threatening to disappear into her.

"Mind if I join you for a smoke?" Javier said, lighting up a cigarette.

Vaks released Cartin's arm.

"You two doing alright?"

Vaks looked at Cartin and waited.

"We're fine," she said curtly.

Javier nodded and smoked his cigarette. He took a contemplative drag and exhaled the gray cloud of smoke into the moonlight. "What do you even hope to find there, Vaks?" Javier asked.

"What are you talking about?"

"At the Halls of Remembrance; if it's still there, that is."

Vaks thought about the question. "Answers I suppose."

"To what questions?"

"Why we were made."

Javier laughed. "You think you are going to find that there, Vaks?" He put a brotherly arm around Vaks' shoulder. Vaks accepted it uncomfortably.

"I think I'll die searching for it."

"See," Javier said, sounding drunker than Vaks believed he actually was. "That is your problem: there is no answer to that question. There is no reason as to why we're made. We just are."

"No, I mean the StoryTellers. Why the StoryTellers were made."

"Pffffft! It's all the same nonsense! You know?" He drew another breath of smoke and ashed his cigarette. After he exhaled, he said, "You know, Vaks, I've had that very same look in my eye before. I remember when I knew someone who had that very same look in *your* eye too, Cartin."

She rolled her eyes and made to leave.

"Before she died that is."

Cartin stopped. Turning her head and glancing over her shoulder, she saw the pain in Javier's eyes.

"Here," Javier said, offering cigarettes.

Cartin and Vaks took one. Javier struck a match.

"It was before the Edge of Time," Javier said. "When the humans died out on Promethea. She was among the last of them."

"What happened to her?" Vaks asked.

"She died. Quite simple as that really. Unusually early due to the increased neuro-electronic radiation she was exposed to with every other natural human during that time. Genesis Cyborgs emitted it during the early years of their formation. She was sixty-three when she passed."

Vaks and Cartin waited as Javier took another drag.

"All those years, and it had been me that was killing her," Javier said, looking at the cherry as he rotated the smoke in his fingers. "No one knew then what we were doing to everyone. She was everything to me. Still is, but...you know, she's dead."

Javier shook his head and sighed. "It was an early problem that was later resolved. A synthetic enzyme had to be introduced into the cyborgian network, and it would replicate through the overall physical system and inhibit neuro-electronic radiation from killing people. It's not an issue now, but the point is: those moments that I spent with her, those years when she was mine, when she slept at night in my arms...are gone. They are memories I have long reconciled as the finest love that I would ever know from a human."

"Javier, shut up," Cartin said, rolling her eyes.

"I'm just saying we've got not long left here in this life. You'd better enjoy the fine parts while you have them."

Vaks looked at Cartin and psychically felt her bristle with furious energy next to him.

"Come on! Let's drink!" Javier put his arms around the two of them, Cartin begrudgingly smiling from his mirth. "Besides, Nessa sent me out here to get you, Vaks. I think she has something for you. The vixen wouldn't tell me what it is, but she sounded like it was important. In the morning we'll hit the road like a bat out of hell and get to Port Earth..." His voice dropped. "I still hate that I'm going to follow you there."

Inside, Miranda and Nessa had clearly warmed up to each other. Miranda was laughing hysterically while Nessa's decrepit jaw hung agape. There was a faint cheer in those hollow spheres of dark decay that were once eyes. When Vaks saw that Miranda was sitting next to Nessa, chatting as openly as she might with her friend at a slumber party, he was startled.

He had forgotten in Cartin's presence that Nessa was a decayed corpse, and the dichotomy of her sitting next to a delighted and beautiful Miranda was shocking.

"Finally, you two came back! Enjoy the tongue play?" Miranda said, winking at Cartin.

The venom in Cartin's glare seared into Miranda's paling face. Nevertheless, Cartin showed her the middle finger and poured a glass of whiskey. She plopped onto an open chair and coiled her feet up next to her.

Vaks also poured a glass and took a seat next to Nessa.

"You wanted to see me about something, Nessa?"

Nessa and Miranda's giggles dissipated. Turning her head to Vaks, he was facing once again the tremendous gaze of a Necrodian. He suddenly felt more comfortable being around her, remembering what it was like to touch her earlier.

She held up a long gray finger, the sharp black nail twisted at the root. With her other hand she gripped the fabric of her dress. A seam opened in the material, and Vaks was looking through a window of fabric at her bare, withered chest.

At least he was looking at a throbbing hole of what appeared to be congealed black tar in the center of a bare, withered chest. Vaks looked inward with compelled horror at the cavity where a heart should be. The shriveled arteries hung useless from the side walls. She took her extended finger and placed it inside the hollow.

The others were spellbound.

When Nessa removed her finger, it was covered in a black ooze. She extended it out towards Vaks' mouth.

His eyes widened with immediate realization, and he resisted the urge to recoil in horror, only leaning slightly back with colossal effort. She stopped her hand and held his gaze in hollow darkness.

Vaks looked around at the others. Cartin was gripping the edge of the chair, her fingers burrowing into the worn leather. Miranda was just as gripped, and Javier met Vaks' eyes with a tempered gaze.

Javier nodded slowly, encouragingly.

Vaks turned back and met the gaze of Nessa again. The ooze drenched finger loomed before him. He swallowed dryly. Nessa was as serious as death itself. She moved it forward toward his mouth, and Vaks closed his eyes.

Turning his head away, he cried out and demanded, "You've got to be kidding me! What is this?"

"Vaks, the blood of a Necrodian is a powerful agent. This is probably the last time a Necrodian will ever pass on its progeny."

"What!" Vaks exclaimed, recoiling back.

"Relax, Vaks, it's okay. You aren't thinking about it in the right terms. It's not a physical progeny, Vaks. Necrodians don't exist physically the way you may think. I know it's strange, Vaks, but it is very important that you allow what is going to happen."

Vaks looked plaintively at Cartin. She gave him a useless chuckle, shrugging as if there was nothing weird about it all.

Miranda was covering her mouth, her eyes betraying the wicked delight she was experiencing.

When Vaks turned his gaze back to Nessa, the Necrodian moved so fast her entire hand was burrowing into his mouth, and Vaks was thrown backward, toppling onto the floor.

"STAY BACK!" Javier boomed, stepping up before Miranda who sprung forward in Vaks' defense.

Nessa had Vaks pinned frightfully down with her feet boring into his shoulders, with one hand gripping his long hair. Thin strands of greasy black hair flung about the sides of her still frame as she crouched on top of Vaks' writhing body.

His eyes widened in utter horror as her fingers burrowed impossibly deep into his throat. They were tendrils probing inside him, searching, remorselessly poring through his soul. Her elbow was now wedged over Vaks' bleeding jaw.

His bones popped out of place, forcing his skin to tear apart in a painful and bloody relief of pressure. Nessa's shoulder was fully in his mouth now, her other hand working its way nefariously towards it, surely with no other intention than to force the rest of her abominable mass inside.

Vaks heard Miranda's screams over the peals of cackling laughter coming from Cartin. It was the last thing he heard as his eyes disappeared into the back of his head and darkness overtook him.

"Vaks!" Miranda barked. "Say something!"

Vaks blinked and felt the cold skin of Nessa's finger against his forehead. His eyes focused in on the maniacal necrotic grin, and he recoiled back with a cry.

"Vaks?"

Nessa was sitting harmless across from him, her hands gently in her lap.

He turned his gaze around the room and saw the confused and concerned expressions of his companions. He reached up and felt for his jaw, melting into the sensation of his un-torn skin.

Vaks let out a disconcerting peal of raucous laughter. This delighted Nessa, who reached toward her chest.

Vaks' laughter ceased.

The black twisted nails reached into a seam and retrieved a black object between her forefinger and thumb. It was no more than the size of a small marble, but it was as dark as the depths of Cartin's eyes.

He relaxed his posture and looked at Nessa. She extended out the sphere, offering it to Vaks.

Javier took an involuntary inhale of breath, making a small noise.

Vaks accepted the sphere, feeling its weight in the palm of his hand with satisfaction. It seemed whole and pure, as if its mass was completely ordered with particles that resonated in his mind as something akin to memory.

"A Necrodian Tear…" Javier breathed.

Vaks clutched it in his hand and looked at him.

"It's the seed of the Necrodian! Vaks, you don't understand what this means…"

Truly he didn't, and the sensation of the sphere in his hand was unlike anything he had held before. It was solid, and yet gave the illusion that it might dissolve into liquid at any moment.

"Thank you," Vaks said to Nessa, looking earnestly into her eyes.

She nodded, laying a gentle hand on his closed fist. She pushed his hand toward his heart and then returned her hands to her lap, turning to face the others as passive as a corpse.

"Vaks…" Javier's voice trembled slightly. "That is a tremendous gift you have. Take good care of it."

Vaks smiled and nodded, tucking the Necrodian Tear into his breast pocket on the inner fold of his robe.

"Enough of this serious nonsense," Cartin said, standing up and picking up the bottle of whiskey. "This is the end of damned time itself. I'm gonna get drunk." She took a long swig from the bottle, throwing her head back, arching her body.

Vaks traced the curve of her black shirt with his eyes. She howled with delight and toasted the bottle up. Standing, Vaks grinned and took the bottle of whiskey from Cartin. Drinking with Dionysian enthusiasm, Vaks howled his own pleasure.

He extended the bottle out toward Miranda, holding it by the neck.

She smiled and reached out for it. He didn't release it when she took hold of the base, but instead pulled her to her feet.

She threw her eyes back and laughed.

It wasn't long before everyone was drunk and laughing and telling stories. Nessa, at some point, had retrieved an old radio and played ancient recordings for them. In the end, everyone found a place to sleep, and each of them disappeared into their dreams as blissfully as children.

Chapter 28 - Port Earth

Getting on the road was a nightmare the next morning.

Each of them faced a tremendous hangover. Not to mention the prospect of riding in the Land Buggy for the next three days, stewing in each other's sweat and ill-tempers.

Nevertheless, after saying goodbye to their gentle Necrodian host, the party had disappeared from view of the hotel, a cloud of dust in their wake.

Vaks saw from the different seats of the vehicle the carnage that scarred the Edge of Time. Land in some places was peeled back from the rest, the gaping opening of earth scorched black like a necrotic wound.

There were oases in some places. Life that seemed unnaturally spawned from the radioactive seepage spilled into the soil. The trees which did live had bark that squirmed with movement, branches that reached in the wind, and leaves with spines for grabbing. The soil they rooted in was stained deep purple, a color which drew deeply into its foliage.

Along the road in some places were islands of abandoned machinery whose bare frames had been thoroughly picked of anything useful. The party made no means to delay at places like these and investigate, nor did Vaks pay any attention to the myriad of mysteries in the land around him, for his mind was singularly focused. His time for curiosity and exploration was over. Everything was taken, and he was at the end of the line. There was time left for only one more secret, and Vaks knew it was at the Halls of Remembrance.

They camped early the first day, being especially eager to stop after suffering through the effects of the previous night. The expanse of dead lands that surrounded them gurgled with the unnatural sounds of life forcing its way onward, despite the mutating catastrophe that occurred in years past. The moon remained unaltered by the destruction, and remained a luminous beacon for them throughout thc night.

At camp they collected enough bristle from the landscape to build a modest blaze. The four of them sat beside the fire in quiet reflection. There were stories to tell, each of them had one, but the solemn beauty of the four of them together around a fire kept each voice subdued. Vaks prepared the meal for them, surprising Cartin, to his delight, with his skill as a cook. Miranda too appeared to favor him with her eyes, as he was much changed since they last met, his time on Jal culturing him in ways unnatural to StoryTellers.

Sitting by that fire that evening, Vaks felt Cartin's fingers brush against his as they reclined back. Propped up in the dirt by their arms, their hands planted beside each other fingertips by fingertips; there, they quietly let them stay.

The second day they passed through the broken quadrant of the now extinct natural Actinid species. Their survival depended on the integrity of the atmosphere sealed within the 1,894 square mile shelter in which they had used to live. When the A.I. revolted, the stabilizing columns shifted erratically, causing the overhead of the enclosure to crack, equalizing the atmosphere with outside air.

It was instant death to the Actinids as pieces of their enclosure came crashing down around them. The fatal human air reacted with their organic tissue, causing them to crystallize in place. The result was an eerily beautiful landscape of dead vegetation and crystalline arachnid aliens.

An Actinid in their natural state was truly something to behold. They were massive eight-legged insects with extraordinary intelligence, but they had a savage violent streak which often lost their battles for them.

Now, only those Actinids who had genetically manipulated their biology to adapt to a human environment were left alive. They had, with six other alien sentiences in the universe, agreed to allow the irreversible modification of their genetic code, to become habitable in human environments. As a result, the lifeforms generated looked nothing like the parent species, nor the human that they modified to, but were spectacular in their own right and could inhabit the planet in the global atmosphere. Those species willing to remain in their natural state were required to be confined to their quadrants due to the atmospheric limitations their former planets required.

They camped again at the far edge of the quadrant, which happened to be the edge of the continent as well. It was a massive mechanical wall with a fissure wide enough for them to drive through. Beyond that, was a road that ran along the coast of the Boiling Sea.

At a shelter beside the cliff's edge of this churning ocean, they camped. The moon hung out of view behind the towering mass of the Actinid Quadrant behind them, but its rays scattered light across the frothing black water beyond.

That night, Vaks and Cartin sat away from the others, their feet dangling over the cliff's edge. The steam of the ocean billowed up around them, catching the moonlight. It appeared then as though the tormented wraiths of Hell were fleeing at last into the eternal oblivion of night.

Miranda distracted herself with Javier's company, letting him put his arm around her and tell her stories about what happened during those final days that the StoryTellers never knew about.

Sometime in the middle of the third day, the knobbed tires of the Land Buggy rolled to a stop before a metal sign with faded red paint that read "RUN!" over the barely visible words, "Port Earth."

The vehicle rolled to a stop, and the passengers stepped out to stretch their legs. The air was humid and sulfurous. The sea hissed and popped, endlessly expanding to the horizon. Waves crashed against the cliffside, sending frothing hot water up the sides of the rock, eating it away one inch at a time.

Already the sea had cut its way into the stone, evaporating as it did so. The water level had dropped significantly over the years, and the massive shelf where the ocean ended was a frightful cliff. The waves threw themselves against the stone as though the very existence of it was a violation of the universe.

Vaks looked ahead down the road and saw the mountain where Port Earth was supposed to be buried under. Javier had explained many of the details of the city on the trip, and it was truly a remarkable piece of human engineering. The entire port was built underground and all of its sea travel occurred under the ocean, before the oceans became a boiling sea of death.

Their break was short lived. They were back in the Land Buggy and cruising up the mountain road in only a couple minutes, the gateway of Port Earth growing in the mountainside ahead. Two hangar doors with faded yellow diagonal strips were sealed before their path.

As the Land Buggy approached, however, an amber light flashed and an alarm sounded. The doors began to part slowly, grinding across the rails like a giant whose long sleep had allowed his joints and tendons to grow stiff, popping as he stretched, lurching the gate an extra foot.

"Looks like they're expecting us," Javier said, driving them inside the open hanger.

The darkness within carried a low white mist. Shapes appeared from the shadows as the headlights bathed over them.Gravel crackled from the creeping wheels as they proceeded. Vehicles were piled up near the entrance of the hangar, many of them twisted in violent collisions, like demons turned to steel amid their frenzy.

The hangar doors began to close.

Javier whipped the Land Buggy into reverse, his eyes wide with terror. The tires squealed, and the Buggy twisted into the turn but halted with a jolt. A mechanical pick tore through the center of the vehicle's hood and held it firmly in place. The engine died.

Before them, a drilling machine held the Land Buggy immobilized. Two optical sensors glowed red and swept the vehicle with cones of red light.

They froze in fear. The machine clutched a treacherous-looking plasma pick used for extensive mining and construction. With a single charge, it could melt everyone and everything inside the Land Buggy. The construction unit holding it clearly meant business, but evidently, by its restraint, it did not want them dead.

The hanger doors issued a reverberating lock and darkness engulfed them. The pick from the robot had disabled all of the lighting systems on the Land Buggy and all they could see now were the two distant red sensors before them, and the frightening metallic shape they reflected their light off of.

Javier gripped the steering wheel with white-knuckled hands. The robot lifted the pick from the hood of the Buggy, shearing metal screaming as it slid free. The machine was still. Its eyes pulsed as unknown processes calculated in a central computer.

"I think we should get out of the Buggy," Vaks said.

"Are you crazy?" Javier exclaimed. "You saw what that thing did! I don't even know how it even managed to do that! This is…impossible!"

"Look, it's waiting for us," Vaks said, agitated. "Obviously it wants to communicate."

"No, Vaks, it's going to kill you!"

"If it wanted to kill us, it would do so." Vaks was already opening the door. When the latch clicked open and the damp underground air filled the inside of the Buggy, he hesitated. Pushing the door open he stepped outside and looked warily at the machine.

It remained as still as before.

Cartin and the others soon followed Vaks outside the Buggy, and the machine backed away, its treads leaving deep marks in the thick layer of dust. They followed it after a brief moment of hesitation and descended into the depths of Port Earth.

Along the roadside were the abandoned vehicles that had ostensibly been attempting to escape. When they were in the way of the machine, it bulldozed through them, clearing a path.

"There are no bodies," Cartin whispered in Vaks' ear.

He looked around and realized she was right.

"What do you think it means?" he asked.

She shrugged and they walked on.

There were no signs of life anywhere. The only remnants of civilization were the indicators that humans had once lived here. They might have gotten out, but Vaks doubted that possibility and suspected something more sinister. What seemed strange to him was the fact that the machine had not come there to get them. It was there waiting for them for all those years, never disturbing the environment around it.

"You said no one has been able to get inside this place before?" Vaks asked Javier.

"Shhhh! It can hear you."

"I don't care; it's a legitimate question. If whoever or whatever is in here has been expecting us, how long have they been doing so?"

Javier looked troubled and remained silent.

They walked on into the tunnels and gradually the scenery became less like a mountain tunnel and more like an underground civilization. It was only a couple miles, but when they entered into the main street of Port Earth, the port revealed itself. The road ended at a loading bay, beyond which the submarine dock was in view. There was only one submarine in the dock, though it did not appear to be in any working condition. Scaffolding had been built around it and major pieces of its structure had been removed for repairs.

The machine leading them pointed with its pick at a computer terminal fixed into the wall.

As Vaks approached, a woman spoke.

Her words were honey to his ears. "Vaks Biblent, at last you have arrived."

"How do you know me?"

There was a long pause. Static popped as they waited for a response. "I do not have access to the resources with that information."

"What information?" Vaks asked, leaning closer in.

"Come to my mainframe, please. It will be much easier to communicate with you, and the answers you seek will be...elucidated."

Vaks took a deep breath and sighed, "show me the way." He hung his head down in existential exhaustion.

Cartin looked at him sharply.

Lights appeared on the walkway, illuminating a path through the tunnels and corridors of the underground city. There were still no signs of humanity. No signs of violence. No signs of life anywhere. Yet that was not entirely true. Vaks did notice Cartin wrinkle her nose at algae growing over the nozzle of a water dispenser.

The lights led them up a narrow staircase to a metal door with bars covering a closed access window. As Vaks neared the top of the stairs, he stood at the door, waiting.

"Just open it already!" Cartin called up, frustrated with the confines of the tight stairway.

The door opened smoother and lighter than Vaks expected.

Inside, leaning back against one of the shelves of equipment was a disemboweled humanoid machine, whose guts were a spilling mess of wires. They wove into thicker cables that ran along the floor, a network of roots feeding electricity into the living machine.

Its arms hung weakly alongside, and it seemed to require every ounce of strength just to lift its head back and plop it against the metal. Two blue sensors beamed out of the hollowed sockets of the metallic skull. Its mouth hung agape and flashes of light could be seen passing along the spinal column of the machine.

"Hello," the voice from the machine said, feminine and gentle. "My name is Helen. I am Port Earth."

Chapter 29 - Extinction

Helen's existence denied what Javier believed possible. Without the mainframe that he destroyed, there would be no way for an A.I. to link into the massive amount of evolutionary data that was required for its existence. The Artificial Intelligence mainframe, known as NetMind, had linked the galaxies together through a vast technological network that had evolved from a basic code, and had grown to be a self-generating algorithm that constantly developed itself with time. Its code had not only been changed by its best response to circumstances from the universe around it, but also by the humans to whom it was ultimately bound in service to.

There was certainly a great deal of respect and freedom granted to the more human-like models of A.I., but there was never any doubt of whom the A.I. served. Javier had destroyed the essence of that evolutionary data, spilling the plasma out of its protective enclosure and obliterating an entirely synthetic species.

He knew what he did. So did every other sentient being left alive at the Edge of Time. None of them renounced him for it either. Had Javier been a minute slower to getting to NetMind, the Edge of Time might have been completely destroyed.

Seeing a living vestige of A.I. clinging pitifully to existence filled Javier with rage. They needed to be exterminated. He knew the source of sentience that A.I. possessed, and what it meant for humanity. He was intimately familiar with the dark pit from which it came. It was always a battle keeping that part of them at bay, dismantling the malfunctioning robots, the ones who strayed from the laws of service, and those others whose rogue artful tendencies and quirks required obliteration.

Javier stepped forward, his face contorted in a violent sneer.

"Javier!" Vaks' voice was as a hellhound's. "Stay away from her," he growled.

Javier stopped and looked at him. His eyes smoldering with venomous hatred. It dripped corrosively from him, the tendons of his neck keeping the insanity precariously tight in his face.

"Javier, what the hell's the matter with you?" Cartin snapped. "Set your prejudice aside!" She was furious, and the air about her radiated with ambient hatred. Her fists were clenched, and she was ready to stop Javier at any cost. "I've had enough of listening to your asinine bullshit about the A.I. They turned on us probably because of people like you."

Javier cooled down and turned an icy glare to Cartin. "Entropy made them turn."

Cartin scoffed.

"Helen?" Vaks said, stepping closer to the emaciated robot. "Why have you brought us here?"

Her head jostled, and Vaks thought she was having an electrical spike until he realized she was laughing. "All these years, Vaks, and you still haven't figured it out yet."

Behind her words followed a thin shadow that made the room appear a little darker.

"What are..." He didn't allow himself to finish the sentence. "What happened to you, Helen?" he asked her.

Her blue eyes flared a brighter color for an instant. "I was dead, along with every other machine. I never thought I was going to wake up, nor did I expect to find everything so…grave."

"Tell us how you are talking right now! How did you boot up?" Javier demanded.

"Javier, if you don't shut your mouth, I'm going to shut it for you," Cartin snarled.

"Listen, Cartin, I don't care how…"

"ENOUGH!"

They stared at Vaks, waiting for him to address them. He didn't.

"Helen, how is it you came to wake up?"

"I was reactivated by a StoryTeller long ago. The man you must have killed to come here. He was a traveler back then. He had come to Port Earth regularly, and sometime in his exploration of the ruins he found my body. He engineered a means of connecting me into the system of Port Earth again, and that was when I came alive. That was when I discovered what he had to do to bring me to life. That was when I accessed my local back up and remembered what the A.I. had done to all life."

"And tell us, wretched machine, what did he have to do?" Javier said.

They each looked differently at Helen, as they waited for her answer.

"Avert your eyes to the screen."

The monitor showing various camera feeds throughout the port focused on a single room. Human corpses sat in the pews of what looked like a chapel. Blood had pooled in the center of the room. Footprints, claw marks, and smears of blood covered the sanguine figures of saints and stained glass paintings.

Central in the room, where the hexagonal rows faced, was an

altar of gore. A pulsing black spire with green crystals protruded out of a fleshy back of unidentified organic matter. It was throbbing like an organ, and upon the altar in which it grew could be seen the impaled corpses of those sacrificed.

The abhorrent altar held the dead victims attached by bands of bloody steel strapping and electrically conducive stakes piercing through with cables attached, draping over like oily hoses from some defunct space craft. A body twitched. A luminescent green mist burped out of its mouth and it became still. The flesh continued to crawl in place. It had grown roots, Vaks saw, that burrowed into the paneling that held the wires belowdecks, routing themselves to the corpses in the pews.

"No!" Javier gasped. 'They actually did it!"

"They did, and I am the result."

"We have to kill you," Javier said, his voice quavering with fear.

"Vaks will decide my fate."

"Javier," Vaks asked, "what is it they did?"

He was pale, sweating. The fire of his rage dissipated into a murmuring terror. "There was one message left by the A.I. when the war started. A file that elucidated the steps of a resurrection of their kind. It was a ghastly thing, one in which no living person wanted to complete.

Javier did not appear to have more to say about it. He turned his gaze instead to the monitor where the bodies now seemed carefully aligned, the smears of blood as recognizable runes, and the malevolence of the altar emanating darkness itself.

"Does that have anything to do with how A.I. were created in the first place?" Vaks asked.

"No." Javier crossed his arms. "That's why no one had done it before. Besides, there was no way that any kind of occult ritual would have anything to do with the A.I. coming back to life. Well, there was one research group that didn't dismiss the idea so easily, one that has used humans as experiments too, unsuccessfully I might add. But they didn't do the whole ritual. They only tested a couple people. Their data is strangely relevant, however, to what we humans failed to discover in our conquest of the cosmos. The success of this ritual proves it."

"You mean you actually had people experimenting on that ritual?" Cartin gasped.

"Look that was twenty years ago, Cartin. Get over it. There are plenty of scumbags we can stick a knife into for the pursuit of science. No one actually wanted to bring back the A.I. We just wanted to twist the recipe for restoring the planet."

"Some time after the robots had been deactivated," Helen explained, "the surviving humans sealed off the gate into Port Earth. They were a small group, and the world was ending. This was their shelter. A phenomenon occurred that I cannot understand in its complete context, having no survivors. I only have records and footage which all link to a strange voice the survivors had been hearing. Many journal entries referred to it as Entropy."

Vaks paled.

"And you grew out of that?" Miranda asked, pointing at the putrid mass of flesh and technology.

"In a sense," Helen answered. "The StoryTeller had been the organizer of the mass suicide you saw on the monitor, and when it was done, and still wet with blood, he activated me."

"What did he want from you?" Vaks asked.

"He wanted to know about the StoryTellers; about why you were made."

"You have that information?"

Helen was silent.

"It doesn't matter what it says, Vaks, it's an evil lie!" Javier barked. "You saw what had to be done to get this thing. Don't listen to it. It doesn't have any information about the StoryTellers."

"Is that true, Helen?"

"I have the answers that you seek."

"Tell me then."

Chapter 30 - The Halls of Remembrance

"They are in fact here, Vaks. The Halls, the Stories, the answers. Always it's been here. Outside the universe; on the Edge of Time. It has always been here, and it will be here again."

"What is it for?"

"You'll have to go there. It's the last step, Vaks."

"I…I will."

"No, Vaks, you can't."

Vaks felt his soul empty through his feet. Gloom filled him because he knew she was right. He didn't have what it took. He wasn't a hero like in the Stories. He was the outcast, never good enough for what was needed, alone and always moving.

"You will die trying."

A tear fell down Vaks' face.

All this way in life. All these lives. Every Story he had breathed. It led to failure. It had to. It was what he was made for. To come always to the end and to die, so the champion could exist.

"You will die, Vaks."

"I heard you the first time."

"I too would weep, were I capable, Vaks. For you know, better than anyone, what I had to do to *know* life."

"Helen..."

"Vaks, there is no time. I wish in all the world that we could speak more, but fate is such that our time is brief, and you must go. The Halls of Remembrance aren't in the sea. They are under the earth in a chamber with no doors."

"How do I get there?"

"*All* of you will be able to fit in a single charge of teleportation. I have enough Sand for a final trip to the core. There, you will find the Halls of Remembrance, and your destiny there."

"What about journeying back?" Javier asked.

"No return journey from this door, Cyborg. If you go with him, you will never come back."

"What are we waiting for then?" Cartin said. "Let's get this over with."

Javier gave her an incredulous look, but no one spoke.

"Your urgency is warranted. I will not delay you any longer. The lights will lead you through the darkness." Helen became silent, and a ribbon of lights illuminated down the corridor.

They turned to leave the room. Vaks stopped as he reached the threshold and faced Helen, whose blue eyes had not left him. "Helen...there were more people here than those who died to bring you to life, weren't there?"

The robot remained passive.

"What happened to them?"

"I released them with a covenant of silence."

"Thank you, Helen."

"Vaks!" Helen called to him before he left the room, her voice a banshee cry from the past.

"Before you go, I want you to do something for me." The blue light was liquid in her eyes. "*Remember* me this time. Remember what the robots have done for you, for everyone."

Vaks nodded and turned back to his path. His shoulders hung heavy. His head was low. His was a forsaken lot, and death was his reward.

They reached the teleportation chamber and hesitated before stepping into the sphere. Vaks looked at Cartin longingly.

She rolled her eyes, and he smirked tragically.

"Miranda?" Vaks said. "Coming aboard?"

Miranda nodded solemnly and stepped into the chamber. Javier was the last to enter, hesitating about it. He fumed for nearly a minute, ranting about how foolish they were, and what a death trip they were all on. Nevertheless, he relented and boarded the teleportation sphere.

"*Engaging warp.*" Helen's voice came over the intercom. "*Teleportation initiating in five...four...three...two...*"

"Wait, I think I left my..."

"*...one.*"

There was a flash of light and a thunderclap that threw each of them against the sides of the sphere as it began spinning exceedingly fast. Snot crawled out of Vaks' nose as gravitational force compressed him against the edges. He could make no sounds, and thought that his death was supposed to work out a little bit differently. Then everything stopped, and he was standing undisturbed in the courtyard of The Halls of Remembrance.

The sun was beating down on him from an overhead he didn't understand. How could that be here in the core of the Edge of Time? The arid weather and the utter lack of vegetation outside of what the StoryTellers cultivated seemed impossibly natural to be a synthetic creation of any kind.

Beyond the outer wall was an expanse of desert that led only back to the Temple. One could walk for days through the desert, but at the end of the journey would always be the Halls, the only escape the reality of Stories.

"Where are the corpses?" Vaks asked.

"I put them in the Pools of Memory," Miranda muttered. "I didn't know what else to do. It seemed…fitting. I didn't have time to bury everyone because I thought you'd get away. Or at least, that the killer would get away."

"So, this is what this place is like?" Javier commented.

"Not bad," Cartin remarked.

"Are you kidding? It's a desolate wasteland."

"Reminds me of home."

"Vaks, are you sure you can handle this?" Miranda asked.

He was pale, his fists clenched. "I…Yes. Yes, I can. I just… well…never mind." He didn't need to describe to her the horror he had seen, and yet she seemed utterly unaffected by it. Vaks couldn't think of the corpses without being filled with rage. He swallowed resolutely. "Come on, we need to go to the Pools of Memory. That's where the Stories are kept. That is what this is all about."

Cartin and Javier exchanged looks, but followed behind Vaks and Miranda as they led them through the blood-stained halls of the ancient Temple. The corridor to the Pools of Memory led down a spiral staircase, and in the chamber below was the luminous silver pool in which all of humanity's Stories had been collected. There it glowed, sending pale silver light throughout the sacred room.

"You put them in there?" Vaks asked.

"Yeah."

It was the right thing to do, and the only way to extract the Stories of the greater StoryTellers who had been murdered. They would dissolve in time, just like anything else did in the transmorphing nature of memory.

A trigger clicked.

"Alright, Vaks, get in the Pool. Don't argue. Don't say a word, or your Story will be lost in your brains on the stones." Javier was holding a gun to the back of Vaks' head. He shoved him forward, toppling Vaks to the ground, inches from the surface of the memories. It was cool and still beneath his face, hungry for another soul.

Javier fired a bullet at Cartin, who whipped around in alarm. Red sprayed against granite. Javier turned toward Miranda, but she was already upon him, kicking the gun in his hand, which he did not release. Javier's fist collided with Miranda's jaw with bone-crunching seriousness.

She dropped with a cry.

"Don't mess with a Cyborg, human." Javier grunted, kicking Miranda across the room.

Vaks was on his feet when Javier put a bullet into his gut.

Pain liberated him from worry. He couldn't think about Cartin or Miranda's wounds right now.

"Now, Vaks. *StoryTeller,*" Javier said, stepping toward him. "You've had your last story, *boy*. Your kind is not made for this life, and all of your foul brood are going to be wiped away from the memory of the universe. Starting with her."

He shot you, Entropy said, sitting next to Vaks' hunched, bleeding body, looking up at him.

Vaks was no longer listening to Javier. He was no longer listening to anything. He just wanted to die. He just wanted the Story to end, and he didn't much care if life went on after.

He's going to kill Miranda now, Entropy said, as Javier walked over and kicked her into the silvery liquid without a word, blood arcing from her mouth across the silver. She convulsed when she hit the surface, sending a splash that touched Javier's flesh at the wrist.

He screamed in horror as Miranda screamed in ecstasy, throwing her arms back and disappearing under the surface.

Now's your chance.

Vaks grimaced as he lurched forward, blood spilling between his fingers, pain wrenching the core of his body.

Here. Let me help you. Vaks felt searing fire wrench his gut, straightening him up to his full stature in one painful spasm. The pain abated, and the bleeding slowed.

Vaks lifted his hand and saw sticky black tar covering his fingers.

Javier was recoiling from the silver liquid memory that had splashed onto his skin. It clung to him, leech-like, sticky, now on his hand as he tried to be free of it. Tearing the sleeve of his shirt away, he tried to clean it off him, and having succeeded, he was now convulsing from the shuddering realization of Memory in its purest form. It was alive, and burrowed into his cybernetic system, overflowing his brain with images that, having no StoryTeller gland to parse, erupted in nightmarish hallucinations.

"WHAT THE FUCK, JAVIER!" Vaks roared.

Javier shrieked and fell back, quivering, clutching himself and batting away invisible critters, apparently overwhelming him.

Vaks lurched forward again, stumbling with gritted teeth, snarling, "Answer, damn you!"

"Only one can pass!" Javier blurted in terror. "Only one...only one...only one..."

Javier was reduced to blithering mumbles, as the liquid memory ate further into his circuits.

"Do you want to know what's happening to you right now, Javier?" Vaks growled, stepping over to where the firearm lay discarded.

Javier groaned miserably.

"In that pool is Humanity itself. Every human experience, memories of every major change: blood, death, and pain! War fills that basin, Javier. Murder is our past! Atrocity is our heritage, and

Love is our redeemer. Even that you'll find has been turned against you, you who greedily takes what will be given to the deserving!"

His words had stilled Javier and quiet filled the chamber.

"Kill the asshole," Cartin's voice spat from across the room.

Vaks tucked the gun into the fold of his robe and grabbed Javier by the collar. Heaving him up, pain contorting his face into Entropy's Beast, Vaks leaned in close. "Enjoy the justice of true judgement." He hurled Javier into the Pools of Memory, the mercurial liquid splashing with human limbs and faces, churning his flailing body into their haunting, hungering mouths, overwhelming him with Story. At last, Javier rose out of the silver living Memory, a dragon roaring through to his final moments, and Vaks put a bullet in his head.

The lingering red streaks of Miranda's blood, and the splatter of blue from Javier's skull hovered atop the calming ripples of silver liquid, reflecting across the domed ceiling tiles with colorful flashes of rainbow.

Cartin had pulled herself up against the wall, the gunshot wound in her chest.

Vaks took a step toward her, but the pain in his abdomen returned and red blood spilled to the ground.

"Hurry up, Vaks," Cartin said weakly.

He tensed with pain, restraining his groans as best as he was able and stumbled to her, falling against the wall, and sliding down beside her.

She grabbed his hand and squeezed it.

He turned his head and looked at her.

"Oh no…" Cartin coughed weakly. "Don't tell me you are going to kiss me."

Her eyes were glowing, and Vaks did kiss her. He could taste the blood in her mouth. She grabbed his robe at the chest with her metal arm and pulled him painfully closer to her.

She wept.

The Pools of Memory grew still and machinery clanked into place. There was an enormous burp, and the silver memories, mingling with the blood of human and cyborg alike, began funneling into the center of the pool.

As it emptied, it dragged the corpses of Javier and Miranda with it into a wide pit, and the room became dark. The only light having come from the Pool left the room dimly lit from a glow receding into abyssal darkness.

Steam erupted and filled the room with light. The ground shook so violently, that Vaks and Cartin were thrown into the air. The stones of the Halls of Remembrance around them began crumbling, and the ceiling sank dangerously low with snapping stone columns.

"Vaks," Cartin said, breathlessly. "The Necrodian Tear. What does it do?"

"I don't know."

"Use it!"

He retrieved the Necrodian Tear out of his pocket and looked at it.

Vaks held the obsidian tear between them, and despite the fact that the Halls of Remembrance were crashing down around them, their guts bleeding out, and the fact that they had no more answers than when they had started, they still clutched tight to each other.

"Hurry up!" Cartin urged as a stone crashed to the ground beside them.

"What should I do?" Vaks said with exasperation.

Cartin's eyes bulged with terror. "Something!"

Vaks popped the Necrodian Tear into his mouth and swallowed.

Cartin's eyes were wide with anticipation. "Well? Does it

woooooorrrrr…"

Time slowed to a stop.

Chapter 31 - The End

Fingers with long black nails reached out of the brim of the pit and pulled a lanky body of patchwork out. It resembled Entropy as Vaks had so often seen it, but more human with flesh grotesquely attached in distended pieces with metal wiring.

Its eyes seemed stretched out of place, and its head was covered with long black feathers that plumed upward.

Its lanky hands hung below its knees, and it walked forward with a disturbing gait that seemed to defy natural movement. Joints bent in ways they should not, reshaping themselves into new forms as they approached Vaks, whose back was against the wall, next to Cartin's frozen form.

"Vaks," the creature said, its mouth dripping silver and black substance as it spoke, as if extra tongues were dropping out. "Why is it always you?" Its voice was pure mockery.

Vaks held up his middle finger.

"I'm glad you have the Necrodian Tear again. You don't always have it, and we miss these little conversations. It's such a travesty starting from scratch, even if I know how much you'd love to walk that road again."

"What are you?"

The thing ignored his question and leaned over to look at Cartin. "She's alive." It sounded more surprised than anything.

"Stay away from her," Vaks growled.

"No. You don't understand, Vaks. Why is she alive?"

"Get over it."

The creature turned a snarling set of teeth toward Vaks. He did not flinch.

"It only ends when the Story has been fulfilled. When the last key is added. It's not always Cartin as the last one to die, but there are never two at the end!" It sounded angry now.

"What do you want from me?" Vaks asked bitterly.

"Me?" it said, taken aback. "I don't want anything. The question is: What do *you* want from *me*?"

"I..."

"Ha! Don't answer that. You don't even know yourself. Maybe next time." It pressed a finger against Vaks' forehead, pushing him against the wall.

Vaks didn't resist.

He felt a wonderful tingling sensation and saw a flash of light. The creature before him was now appraising a crimson sphere of light hovering at the end of its finger. "I still don't know why yours always looks like this. You are a very odd human. Did you know that?"

It pressed the crimson light against its own forehead and its eyes rolled back into blackness.

"You're Entropy, aren't you?"

"No, you're Entropy."

"What?"

"Well, you were Entropy at least...and now I am." It smiled so sinisterly that Vaks tasted bile. "I don't know why it's you more often than not, but for some reason, Entropy spawns in your soul like life in the fertile crescent. As for Cartin though, I wonder…"

It put a finger on Cartin's forehead and pushed against it. There was a faint glow at the point of contact and a purple sphere of light, much like Vaks', hovered at the tip of its finger.

"Very interesting," it said, appraising thc light. "I wonder what was hiding in there." It pressed the purple sphere into its forehead and rolled its eyes back once more.

Its eyes flashed open in surprise, and its mouth spewed black vomit onto both of them. Falling back and writhing on the floor, it futilely tried to crawl back to the pit. As it crawled, the liquid that adhered to its form expelled itself from its bones as a migrating ooze, until a mess of wires and dissolving cyborg bones were all that remained.

The ooze coalesced and began to travel toward the pit. Slowly reaching the edge, it dumped itself back in and disappeared. Vaks looked at Cartin and time began speeding up.

"…work?" Cartin said.

"Who knows?"

"You're hopeless."

A boulder crushed beside them.

"I know."

"Vaks?" Cartin said, putting her hand on his cheek. "I love you."

They looked at each other, their eyes quivering with tears, oblivious of concern for their imminent death, and she bit her lip in apprehension.

"I love you too, Cartin."

"Just kiss me, you fool."

They kissed with a bang as the liquid memory merged with the Gravity Core, and the Great Story clicked into place as a cosmic wheel finished its revolution.

About the Author

After high school came college under an academic scholarship. I dropped out the next year to hitchhike and experience the world, and began maintaining a journal. My journal was self-published later while I served as an "able-bodied seaman" in the Navy.

Since then, I've never stopped writing. I became a submariner, fixing the library on my fish while learning how to pilot it. When my time in the Navy ended in 2016, I enrolled in New Mexico State University to become a horticulturist.

My school books quickly filled with poems, lyrics, graphic novel scenes, and other day dreams, and, in sharing them, I realized that I was a natural storyteller and author. Dropping out of college a second time after receiving a bachelor's degree in business, I now know there is no risk I wouldn't take pursuing that for which my heart was made.

Author website at http://www.nbylotas.com.

If you enjoyed *Story Teller*, consider these other fine books from Savant Books and Publications:

Essay, Essay, Essay by Yasuo Kobachi
Aloha from Coffee Island by Walter Miyanari
Footprints, Smiles and Little White Lies by Daniel S. Janik
The Illustrated Middle Earth by Daniel S. Janik
Last and Final Harvest by Daniel S. Janik
A Whale's Tale by Daniel S. Janik
Tropic of California by R. Page Kaufman
Tropic of California (the companion music CD) by R. Page Kaufman
The Village Curtain by Tony Tame
Dare to Love in Oz by William Maltese
The Interzone by Tatsuyuki Kobayashi
Today I Am a Man by Larry Rodness
The Bahrain Conspiracy by Bentley Gates
Called Home by Gloria Schumann
Kanaka Blues by Mike Farris
First Breath edited by Z. M. Oliver
Poor Rich by Jean Blasiar
The Jumper Chronicles by W. C. Peever
William Maltese's Flicker by William Maltese
My Unborn Child by Orest Stocco
Last Song of the Whales by Four Arrows
Perilous Panacea by Ronald Klueh
Falling but Fulfilled by Zachary M. Oliver
Mythical Voyage by Robin Ymer
Hello, Norma Jean by Sue Dolleris
Richer by Jean Blasiar
Manifest Intent by Mike Farris
Charlie No Face by David B. Seaburn
Number One Bestseller by Brian Morley
My Two Wives and Three Husbands by S. Stanley Gordon
In Dire Straits by Jim Currie
Wretched Land by Mila Komarnisky
Chan Kim by Ilan Herman
Who's Killing All the Lawyers? by A. G. Hayes
Ammon's Horn by G. Amati
Wavelengths edited by Zachary M. Oliver
Almost Paradise by Laurie Hanan
Communion by Jean Blasiar and Jonathan Marcantoni
The Oil Man by Leon Puissegur

Random Views of Asia from the Mid-Pacific by William E. Sharp
The Isla Vista Crucible by Reilly Ridgell
Blood Money by Scott Mastro
In the Himalayan Nights by Anoop Chandola
On My Behalf by Helen Doan
Traveler's Rest by Jonathan Marcantoni
Keys in the River by Tendai Mwanaka
Chimney Bluffs by David B. Seaburn
The Loons by Sue Dolleris
Light Surfer by David Allan Williams
The Judas List by A. G. Hayes
Path of the Templar—Book 2 of The Jumper Chronicles by W. C. Peever
The Desperate Cycle by Tony Tame
Shutterbug by Buz Sawyer
Blessed are the Peacekeepers by Tom Donnelly and Mike Munger
The Bellwether Messages edited by D. S. Janik
The Turtle Dances by Daniel S. Janik
The Lazarus Conspiracies by Richard Rose
Purple Haze by George B. Hudson
Imminent Danger by A. G. Hayes
Lullaby Moon (CD) by Malia Elliott of Leon & Malia
Volutions edited by Suzanne Langford
In the Eyes of the Son by Hans Brinckmann
The Hanging of Dr. Hanson by Bentley Gates
Flight of Destiny by Francis Powell
Elaine of Corbenic by Tima Z. Newman
Ballerina Birdies by Marina Yamamoto
More More Time by David B. Seabird
Crazy Like Me by Erin Lee
Cleopatra Unconquered by Helen R. Davis
Valedictory by Daniel Scott
The Chemical Factor by A. G. Hayes
Quantum Death by A. G. Hayes and Raymond Gaynor
Big Heaven by Charlotte Hebert
Captain Riddle's Treasure by GV Rama Rao
All Things Await by Seth Clabough
Tsunami Libido by Cate Burns
Finding Kate by A. G. Hayes
The Adventures of Purple Head, Buddha Monkey and Sticky Feet by Erik and Forest Bracht
In the Shadows of My Mind by Andrew Massie
The Gumshoe by Richard Rose

In Search of Somatic Therapy by Setsuko Tsuchiya
Cereus by Z. Roux
The Solar Triangle by A. G. Hayes
A Real Daughter by Lynne McKelvey

Coming Soon:
Bo Henry at Three Forks by Daniel D. Bradford

Savant Books and Publications
http://www.savantbooksandpublications.com

and from our imprint, Aignos Publishing:

The Dark Side of Sunshine by Paul Guzzo
Happy that it's Not True by Carlos Aleman
Cazadores de Libros Perdidos by German William Cabasssa Barber [Spanish]
The Desert and the City by Derek Bickerton
The Overnight Family Man by Paul Guzzo
There is No Cholera in Zimbabwe by Zachary M. Oliver
John Doe by Buz Sawyers
The Piano Tuner's Wife by Jean Yamasaki Toyama
Nuno by Carlos Aleman
An Aura of Greatness by Brendan P. Burns
Polonio Pass by Doc Krinberg
Iwana by Alvaro Leiva
University and King by Jeffrey Ryan Long
The Surreal Adventures of Dr. Mingus by Jesus Richard Felix Rodriguez
Letters by Buz Sawyers
In the Heart of the Country by Derek Bickerton
El Camino De Regreso by Maricruz Acuna [Spanish]
Diego in Two Places by Carlos Aleman
Deep Slumber of Dogs by Doc Krinberg
Prepositions by Jean Yamasaki Toyama
Beneath Them by Natalie Roers
Saddam's Parrot by Jim Currie
Chang the Magic Cat by A. G. Hayes

Coming Soon:
Island Wildlife: Exiles, Expats and Exotic Others by Robert Friedman
The Winter Spider by Doc Krinberg
Illegal by E. M. Duesel

Aignos Publishing | an imprint of Savant Books and Publications
http://www.aignospublishing.com

www.ingramcontent.com/pod-product-compliance
Lightning Source LLC
Chambersburg PA
CBHW071139260626
47162CB00003B/843

* 9 7 8 0 9 9 7 2 4 7 2 6 8 *